Subtle Bodies

NORMAN RUSH

Subtle Bodies

Alfred A. Knopf · New York · 2013

THIS IS A BORZOI BOOK
PUBLISHED BY ALFRED A. KNOPF

www.aaknopf.com

Knopf, Borzoi Books, and the colophon are registered trademarks
of Random House, Inc.

Grateful acknowledgment is made to The Sheep Meadow Press for
permission to reprint an excerpt from "Men on Earth" from the The
Voice of Robert Desnos: Selected Poems, by Robert Desnos, translated
by William Kulik. Reprinted by permission of The Sheep Meadow Press,
Clinton Corners, New York.

Library of Congress Cataloging-in-Publication Data
Rush, Norman.
Subtle bodies / By Norman Rush. — 1st Edition.
pages cm
"This Is a Borzoi Book."
ISBN 978-1-4000-4250-0 (hardcover)   1. Reunions — Fiction.
2. Friendship — Fiction.   3. Marriage — Fiction.   I. Title.
PS3568.U727S83 2013
813'.54—dc23   2013013813

Jacket photograph by Matthew Brooks / Trunk Archive
Jacket design by Gabriele Wilson
Manufactured in the United States of America

FIRST EDITION

For Elsa:
I hope you like being indispensable,
because nothing can be done about it.

Subtle Bodies

1 Genitals have their own lives, his beloved Nina had said at the close of an argument over whether even the most besotted husband could be trusted one hundred percent faced with the permanent sexual temptations the world provided. It was the kind of conversation that went with the early days of a marriage, of their marriage. He had been rebutting her silly but fiendish thought experiments and had gotten tired of the game. She was a genius at imagining inescapable sex traps. There could be a nun suffering from hysterical blindness that would probably become permanent unless she received a sacrificial screw from somebody's husband, alas. He looked around. Good thing there were no nuns on the plane, at least none in costume. When you're traveling you're nothing, until you land, which is what's good about it, Ned thought.

2 Nina, riding in furious pursuit, felt like bucking in her seat to make the plane go faster through the night. She was still enraged. She felt like a baby. She thought, You are a baby: no, he is, he is, my lamb.

Maybe the matronly pleasant-seeming woman sitting next to her was *wise*. She was old enough to be. Anything was possible. And it might not hurt to talk to an adult other than my incessant mother, she thought. She had to call her mother when they landed, first thing. It's just that she won't shut up about my pregnancy, she thought. Her *attempted* pregnancy, was what she meant. She regretted telling her mother about it.

I love my mother, she wanted to tell the woman next to her. It was just that her mother was overflowing with pregnancy lore that had nothing to do with reality. She'd been unkind when her mother said, You smell differently when you're pregnant, because she'd said in response, Oh really? How *do* you smell then? With your uterus? All her mother had been trying to say was that there was a change in the odor a woman's body gives off during pregnancy. But then her mother regularly declared that there was a mystical "subtle body" inside or surrounding or emanating from every human being and that if you could see it, it told you something. It told you about the essence of a person, their secrets, for example. It was all about attending closely enough to see them. They varied in color and brightness. Her mother claimed she could see them, faintly. She wanted Nina not to be oblivious to the subtle bodies of the people she met. That would protect her from *deceivers*, whoever they might be. Ma suggested Ned be on the qui vive also.

Dinner, as they called it, was done with. She seemed to have twisted her napkin into a rope and she wondered if her seatmate had noticed. The woman wasn't being especially friendly to her. Usually the people she happened to sit next to were.

Yes, she was enraged at Ned, but also felt sorry for him. May God help you my lad, my Ned, she thought. He would be dumbfounded when he realized she had sprung after him, done it, like that, like a savage beast dropping everything herself, the same as he had, like a child, an adolescent, a child. He had never seen her truly furious, never once in three years of marriage. He had seen her agitated, and he had seen her annoyed, but never this. I am war, she thought.

No question he deserved tenderness, which he got. On her own, she had quit referring to his beloved clique of college friends as clowns. He hadn't asked her to, but the term had stung him, a little. And this despite the fact that they *had* been clowns manqué, a troupe, goofing on the world under the baton of their maestro Douglas.

She had to control herself. She needed to be calm and alkaline. She thought, I wonder if he thinks I love taking Clomid and standing on my head après sex, with him holding my feet in the air. He had left her a barely readable note. Twice since leaving he'd called her, and each time she'd answered, I am not answering this phone.

*Every*thing had been left for her to deal with, not only everything involving the nonprofits, not only the mis-sent invoices and the complaints about the metallic aftertaste of the coffee they were getting from their co-ops in Belize, but calls about the demonstration he was organizing, the *same* calls over and over again, because this was a *coalition*. She *hated* coalitions. And why did Ned have to be the Chair? She made an involuntary flinging-out gesture that startled her seatmate, who flinched. Nina tried to bury the gesture in a show of policing her tray table. She doubted that the woman was deceived. Ned could be annoying without *meaning* to. Talking about getting pregnant he had said, about his own attitude to it, I can't decide whether I'm ambivalent or not. Which was a ghostly survival of the talky badinage-based humor of his circle of clowns, by which she meant friends, sorry. It was a slightly funny thing for him to say, but the *subject* wasn't funny.

Nina had the window seat. She raised the window shade to study the night. Why did stadiums where no one was at play have to be lit up like Christmas, why? But why everything, really, and why had that woman writing her up in the *Contra Costa Times* described her as sharp-featured, why? Because she wasn't. And why hadn't the woman mentioned her award in the story saying that she was the best accountant the nonprofits in the Bay Area had ever heard of? She considered her reflection in the window. Why not *angular*, instead of sharp-featured?

Well she was going to take the bull by the horns and talk to her co-passenger. It was ordained that the woman's wallet was going to be exploding with snapshots of unblemished grandchildren. She would deal with it. She needed to talk. She needed to be with Ned, *now*, before the thirty-six hours were up, so they could do it. Had he forgotten or did he just not care? About family making, he did feel old for it sometimes. He was forty-eight.

The woman beside her opened her purse and extracted a paperback, which she seemed to be handling rather reverently, like a missal. Nina was curious. The woman moved unsubtly away, taking her elbow off the common armrest.

Nina entertained the idea that the woman had sensed a core truth about her, which was that she always wanted to know what people were reading. I can't help it, she thought. She always wanted to know. It had been embarrassing from time to time when people saw her craning around inappropriately to get a clue about what they were reading. It was just that knowing made her feel better. Somebody could be reading *Mein Kampf*. And she didn't like people who covered the books they were reading in little homemade kraft paper jackets. She couldn't help taking that as a challenge, apparently. Definitely the woman was getting tense. But she might as well relax, because Nina already *knew* what she was reading. She had figured it out in a glance. But I'm clumsy, she thought. Anxious, she thought it again. Then she passed her hands down her sides, for no reason.

The woman had bent the front cover of the paperback around to conceal the spine, and now she was slanting the book so that Nina would be required to contort herself to make out what was on the page. The woman's dual mission seemed to be to read and at the same time keep what she was reading secret from Nina. It was silly because the cover art featuring embossed foil bolts of lightning and a cross on a blood-red field declared that the book was an entry in the genre of Christian theological thrillers that had gotten so popular. That was the last thing Nina needed to think about, the end of the world. Well, she couldn't interrupt this person when she was reading. Because reading was sacred. It *was* to my mother, she thought. The number of times her mother had found her reading intently when it was time to set the table, and given her a pass, was legion.

She wouldn't mind getting into an argument on Christianity. Because she had a new standpoint on the subject since she had happened to marry a sort of Jesus, a secular Jesus, of course, not that Ned would tolerate that description. So far as she knew, he had never done a bad thing, except for like a complete asshole going to the funeral of fucking Douglas, the world's greatest friend—going and just leaving her a few messages. Douglas, never Doug, the rule for addressing the world's greatest friend.

Nina had her own reading matter but she was too hyper to read. Two poems in *Poetry* magazine had irritated her. In one poem, the gist was that the reader goes to the seaside, and it's the sea shouting Help! the sea saying Help! to humans, something like that. And then in another one, the poet seemed to say It's closing time in the old fort and you have to go and you can't find your sons, so what to do, you just go back to the cannons and you'll find them hanging around there. Everything was upsetting. And there was nothing interesting about the interior of a plane. Her seatmate swallowed a cough. Planes were unsanitary. She was breathing recirculated air, and it was Ned, his impulsiveness, Ned, who was to blame. Her fury was rising again.

She knew why it was. Things she wanted, things she thought she had, being jerked away from her without warning and at the last minute, always upset her, based on patterns in her absurd childhood, patterns she had studied and parsed and studied until she was sick unto death of the subject. But her therapist had been a Freudian, and being sick and tired of it wasn't a reason for letting go of something. The reverse! And after years of staring at the facts, she had no idea, still, how she should feel about her pixie parents—up, down, sad, send them to the firing squad? How should she feel about the elf shoes, with their pointy toes curving back toward her little shins, that her mother had gotten on sale, making her wear them to school, insisting they were perfectly normal? She remembered the giant celebration her parents had given when her father finally got into the Screen Extras Guild, in his fifties, was that sane? She had no idea. They did this, they did that. For any ailment, they medicated her with bark tea. Her mother had become an astrologer because it was such a *portable* occupation. But then they had stayed stuck in Los Angeles forever. Linda, her mother's best friend and worst influence, had branched out into astrology for pets, dogs mainly, and tried to get Ma to take it up, which she hadn't.

But then finally, late in the day, turning thirty-four, she had found Ned, and gradually gotten him to want a child, and to really try, with her. And then this. She thought, *I* take the pills, *I* get the shot, *he* vanishes! It was outrageous.

It all had to do with le grand Douglas. Douglas had been the head of Ned's clique in the seventies, the spokesmodel, when they were undergraduates, which would make it Douglas's clique, actually. They had been a group of wits, in their opinion, of superior sensibilities of some kind, was the idea. Everything she knew about Douglas was irritating. He even had his own term for the effect they were going for: perplexion. So elegant. And there was his legendary pensiveness, the way he would sometimes hold up his hand in a certain way to signal the group to stop talking so he could finish a thought he wasn't sharing. Then he might jot something down on a scrap of paper or he might not. The point, to her, seemed to be to show that whatever was going on around him was subordinate to the great private productive   secret-not-necessarily-related-to-anything-his-groundling-friends-were-talking-about trains of thought that Douglas was having.

And one thing she could not get out of her mind was that when Douglas had been the ringmaster of the group at NYU he had demonstrated that he was the world's champion of walking out of the Thalia, walking out on foreign films he personally found highly overrated and taking his pack of stupid fool friends along with him. She had been incredulous, hearing about that, and about Ned *obeying* Douglas, essentially. And Ned had told her about the group going to see *Last Tango in Paris*. And Maria Schneider and Marlon Brando were having precoital fooling around and in the course of it she has to pee and she goes into the toilet in the vacant apartment they're carousing in and the camera follows her and she pees but gets up without wiping or using a bidet or anything and then they had gone on to have sex. So quelle horreur and that was enough for Douglas, who found the hygienic omission a good enough excuse to lead his minions out immediately. His position had been that the omission fatally attacked the plausibility of the scene. They had been very severe about cinema, Ned's group. It was amazing to her. They had walked out on Brando at his professional and physical peak. So why had they kept going to the Thalia led by someone who was so sensitive that half the time their money would be spent for nothing?

And what she did know with certainty was that Ned had been abandoned, abandoned gradually, and then finally, by this man he was racing ahead of her and her ova to praise and bury, and it had been *painful*, muted but painful, to Ned, over the years. And she knew that the abandonment had gotten more painful for Ned as Douglas got half-famous in the world, debunking forgeries, *significant* forgeries. And Douglas had remained closer, Ned had known for a fact, to the other three friends. She had no idea what had led Douglas into the "questioned documents" business, but something had, and he'd made it pay. He'd proved that some sensational papers revealing that Alfred Dreyfus was in fact guilty of espionage were right-wing forgeries. And then someone had forged Milan Kundera's so-called *Love Diaries*, and Douglas had shot that down. And then he had married the leading gossip columnist in Czechoslovakia, the radiant Iva, a consensus great beauty. And he had gotten her over to the U.S. and put her in a tower in the woods, in the Catskills, near Woodstock. And they had lived in it, and there had been an inheritance, and when the internet came, there would be little fragments from Douglas to Ned, avant-garde tips on nutrition or postings from the Committee for Ethical Tourism which proved there was nowhere in the world you could go for a vacation except possibly Canada. She had always wanly hoped to get revenge on Douglas. Because there *had* truly been a superior soul in their little grouplet, and that had been Ned, her lad, her Ned. And there was another thing that had driven her crazy about Douglas. At first through the mail, and then by fax, and then by email, had come a stream, a very intermittent stream, of short papers and notes from Douglas, who had become eccentric and was proposing various universal solutions to the problem of the persistence of evil in the world, in human relations. And some of them had been items like monotheism, and then it had been declining terrestrial magnetism, and there had been others. Like his theory that gradual anoxia was driving mankind crazy, based on the shrinking percentage of oxygen in the atmosphere compared to the much higher oxygen content in air samples taken from bubbles in ancient Egyptian glassware. And then it had been estrogens and antidepressants infiltrating the water supply. Of course it would be very nice if someone could prove that unkindness was caused by pollution.

And Ned had always been dutiful and sent some sort of reply trying to argue, shorter and shorter replies, because Douglas almost never, and then never, had had anything to say to Ned in return, no expansion on the particular subject.

Douglas's group had thought very highly of itself. They were going to be social renovators of some unclear kind, had been the idea, by somehow generalizing their friendship. Ned could still get solemn, talking about those times. She didn't get it. And part of the original group idea had been that they would always be a unity, helping each other, maybe creating a compound in the wildwood for summer vacations or maybe crafting some excellent retirement collective. *Right*, she thought.

One thing she knew and Ned did not, was that there is no permanent friendship between men, among men. Something goes wrong, somebody marries the wrong person, somebody advances too fast, somebody converts, somebody refuses good advice or bad advice, it didn't matter. It went up in a flash, it went up in a flash like magnesium paper set on fire in a magic show. She thought, It's not always great with women, either, but it can be. Women *can* have friends, it's more personal, she thought. Although in the great design of things, women were getting to be more like men. There were more tough cookies around, and liars.

Well, Ned was her friend, her deep friend. He didn't realize it, exactly. He thought everything was love with them, but it wasn't. She would have been his friend whenever. It was a standard fantasy when you fell in love to imagine you could go back in time and find your beloved growing up, appear there, save him or her, get together as adolescents, by magic, and go on together, fighting for one another, into old age, never wavering. It was a pure friendship fantasy. Not sexual.

And that was why she was enraged at the man, enraged. She had to get this rage out of her, so she could kill him when she caught up with him. He was an idiot. He was reckless. He was hopeless. He had shit for brains. He couldn't be counted on. He was a fool. These people had hurt him in the past, Douglas had. She only knew some of it.

She was moving around too much in her seat. The woman next to her was unhappy.

She offered the woman her uneaten dessert, an industrial brownie still in its packaging. Nina had watched the woman devour her own brownie in two bites, earlier.

"No," said the woman, quite forcefully.

She thinks I'm affiliated with Satan, Nina thought.

3 His great friend was dead.

Ned wanted to embrace his dead friend. An imaginary burning feeling ran across Ned's chest and down his arms. He wanted to embrace his friend. Where Douglas's body was, even, Ned didn't know. No clue whether it had been removed from the estate, no clue what shape it might be in wherever it was. Nobody could have gotten there from the West Coast any faster than he had. And still he was late. Except that when the call had finally come from Elliot, it had already been too late, whatever he meant by that. He meant something. Your thinking is choppy, he thought.

Douglas had died when his riding mower had pitched him down into a ravine, the mower on top of him, when the ground at the edge had given way. So he had been buried once already.

These were the Catskills, all around. The upward road he was walking on ran through terrain jammed with trees still dripping from a monster rainstorm he had just missed. It was trees, trees, and glimpses of hills farther off, also burdened with trees, as Douglas might have put it. The ruts in the unpaved road were running like brooks. It was all uphill. There were regular trees in their last leaf, intermixed with unwelcoming, bristling evergreens. It was four in the afternoon.

It was muggy. This was not where he would choose to die, in a ditch in this vicinity. What had Douglas seen, dying, his neck broken and mud sliding over him? No friend near, no one around, black mud engulfing him.

Ned shrugged off his rucksack and, holding it against his chest to give his shoulders a break, continued on. He had brought too much reading matter and had so far only managed to get cursorily through three recent issues of *The Economist*. That had been during the San Francisco–to–Houston leg of the trip, before guilt had shut him down. He was agitated about the war that was coming and guilty that he'd been forced to drop the little he was doing in the effort to stop it. There was going to be a march—the Convergence was what they were calling it—to protest the rush toward war in Iraq. It was looking immense. Feeder marches from all over Northern California would culminate in San Francisco. Contingents were coming from as far north as Yreka, for Christ's sake. There was a coalition for the Convergence, *his* coalition. It was funny, the anarchists were the easiest to deal with and the Quakers were the most difficult. Oh and of course he felt like shit about leaving Nina with so little notice, and leaving exactly when the timing on their personal project was so critical. He couldn't think about that.

4 He had come to a rude plank bridge across a gully occupied by a roaring brown torrent. Spray was coming up through gaps in the planking. The bridge meant that he was better than three-quarters of the way up the road to Douglas's estate. He supposed it had to be called an estate. It did, after all, have a whole variety of buildings on the property, including a stone tower. And this had to be the bridge that some of the taxi services in the area would go no farther than when delivering visitors to Douglas's. He had been given this piece of information by the Trailways driver when he dropped Ned on the highway between his scheduled stops. The driver had also mentioned the tower, and, overall, that the locals didn't like Douglas, or hadn't liked him.

Ned started across the bridge and then stopped. It came to him strongly that he needed a better idea of how he looked before he arrived, and there was no sign of a mirror in the roadway. His eyes itched. *Visine*, he needed. There was none in his toiletries. In fact, his toiletries amounted to a toothbrush and deodorant picked up in an airport shop.

Maybe he looked all right. He was wearing a new tan corduroy hacking jacket, a good blue dress shirt straight from the cleaners. Nina had found the jacket in a Junior League thrift shop she surveilled like a spy. He had all his hair, curly, graying, but still. Somebody in their group, he couldn't remember who, had said it was a fact of life that people tended not to take people with curly hair seriously. But curly or not, he had his hair. He remembered that it was Douglas who had made the crack about curly hair. My weight is okay, one seventy-two is good, he thought. The Timberland boots he was wearing gave his five ten and a half a little help. Elliot was the tallest in their group, six four and an ectomorph. The boots had been purchased by Nina and never worn. She had a mission to get everything together they would need when they went camping at Stinson Beach. They were going to be serious about camping. They had gone once. Stinson Beach was a good choice for starters because it wasn't that far from Berkeley. So camping there could fit neatly into weekends and not protrude into their insane work life. They wouldn't burn up hours getting to where they were going to rusticate.

He kept calling Nina. At some point she was going to talk to him. And she would forgive him. Because she was forgiving. She would be getting deluged with calls for him, emails, faxes.

He should have brought a novel, plucked something from Nina's shelves of uppermiddleclassics. She called them that. Something by Louis Auchincloss or Barbara Pym or Frederick Buechner or Thornton Wilder, people he was not uninterested in reading. He felt guilty over not reading a piece of worthwhile fiction when the constraints of travel made it a completely justifiable waste of time, which was not what he meant. He should have brought along something with a story to it. Well, he hadn't. And he hadn't really tried to pay attention to the Ulster County countryside, either. Why Douglas had chosen to settle in this particular part of the forest was a question. The bus trip had been a montage interrupted by naps and daydreaming: sharp hills, thick forests crowding down close to the road, motels and restaurants and trailer parks, an inner-tubing center, a splatball drome, gun shops, a pottery studio with a huge stucco golem in front holding a sign saying Feats of Clay. A lot of the businesses seemed to be shuttered. It was the end of September. Maybe everything was seasonal. And on the subject of not paying attention, he remembered a couple of years ago when they had been flying over the Rockies on a brilliant clear day and he had chided Nina for not paying attention to the grandeur below and she had said I find scenery beautiful but repetitive.

He was at a halt, there at the bridge. His pant cuffs were drenched dark. He was forty-eight. Of the friends who would be there, Gruen was the youngest. Nina was thirty-seven. He would be meeting Douglas's widow for the first time. She would be a wreck. Douglas's son was fourteen, and Ned had met him briefly when he was a toddler. Elliot would be there, stooping down for embraces, and Joris, all of them.

He was hesitating. He wanted to go back down to the general store. It seemed urgent.

He needed to hurry. There could be more rain. The forest didn't offer much prospect of shelter. Visible here and there among the trees were boulders, huge and mottled with great scabs of lichen. A little lichen goes a long way, he thought. As shelter, the boulders were irrelevant.

He was proud of his life but he wasn't enjoying it as much as he should. The thought surprised him. It was his own formulation, not an echo of a quote. It was probably true a lot of the time. Recently, though, he couldn't complain.

He turned back.

5 This was a store Douglas must have frequented for years. The Vale, it was called. It was clearly from the nineteen twenties or so, a shrine to the period, in its way. The signage said they sold Sundries, along with Bait, Lotto, News, Coffee, and Adult.

The Vale was a collection of disparate buildings populating a flat, boggy strip of land fronting the highway. Going up, Ned had skirted the place. If he'd known he was going to come back down, he could have parked his rucksack at the place. He liked his Swiss Army–issue rucksack. He liked carrying the rucksack of an army that had never fought a war. His enjoyment of that fact was enough to outweigh the pack's unwieldiness.

The Vale's centerpiece was the general store, a barn-like log structure set on an unusually high stone foundation, with verandas along the sides and a deep front porch on which was arrayed a miscellany of seating—barstools, a piano bench, a porch glider, car seats, a church pew. A cinderblock annex housed a propane sales and service operation. Adjoined to that was a decommissioned sky-blue double-wide trailer connected to the annex by an improvised tunnel formed by stretching plastic sheeting over a succession of metal arches. Strings of ancient faded blue-and-yellow Grand Opening pennants encircled the three buildings at the roof line, drawing the elements of the Vale together. Western music and occasional indications of hilarity leaked from the trailer.

Ned set foot on the broken lattice of planks and duck-board that had been laid out on the mud in front of the store entrance. Splendid single lodgepole pines stood at the four corners of the general store. Ned had observed, coming down the mountain, that the personal hinterland of the Vale was essentially a dump site for derelict machinery and other ejecta—there were cairns of hubcaps, short columns of discarded tires, piles of scrap lumber, huge bins wreathed in vines.

Ned mounted the front steps. He stepped into a fluorescent blaze. He felt at first that he was alone in all the light and music of the cavernous establishment. Nina called fluorescent lighting lighting for robots. Music from a ballroom dancing exhibition showing on a TV set fixed high in an angle of the room contended with pop singing from someplace else. A police scanner interjected occasionally. The pop music was, he saw, due to a radio on the checkout counter behind which someone was sitting and watching. Ned had missed him initially because he was half hidden by the monumental antediluvian cash register and he was seated in a wheelchair.

The place was packed with things. Shelving rose almost to the ceiling. The aisles were narrow. Overhead a web of clothesline had been strung, to which articles like swim fins, butterfly nets, snorkel tubes, packs of sparklers, and saw blades had been clipped. An umbrella stand held a collection of gripsticks to be used for securing items from the web or the top shelves. In urgent printing, the sign on the container warned that these devices should be used only with the help of staff, and that any injury, damage, or product breakage resulting from unsupervised use would be the sole responsibility of the customer. There seemed to be no organizing principle: a display case contained fantasy knives and stuffed animals. A rotatable cylindrical rack bore condoms, sunglasses, shrink-wrapped jerky, and pink plastic cap guns. He had to conquer his distraction. He needed to be a customer if he was going to use the toilet. He had to buy something. All of the newspapers that were left were local. But he needed . . . *Visine*. And he needed a comb. He needed to check himself out before the encounter with his friends. Ridiculously, that was why he had turned around on the road and come back to this place. Men weren't allowed to carry pocket mirrors around with them.

He approached the cashier, a delicate old man, handsome, with perfect silver hair, someone who could be a spokesman for dignified old age, except of course that he was in a wheelchair. On closer inspection, he seemed to be a mouth breather. Tacked to the wall behind the old man was a POW/MIA flag showing a GI prisoner, in silhouette, hunched over in dejection. Ned took off his rucksack and set it down where the old man could see it, to reassure him.

"Hello," Ned said, suppressing an impulse to extend his hand to this person who was so neatly gotten up. He was wearing a starched dress shirt buttoned to the neck, a red cardigan without a spot on it, and he gave off a pleasant scent of aftershave. Ned knew what the man reminded him of. He was the patrician Dutchman, the old burgomaster, or even Count, who stands up to the Nazis in a movie written by Lillian Hellman.

Ned said, "I wonder if you have Visine. Eye drops. And a pocket comb."

"*Acourse*," the old man said. So not the patrician, then, Ned thought.

Ned was directed to the bottom shelf where the Visine should be. It was somewhere among the goods in the shelving directly opposite the cashier. Ned understood that there would be another place to look if the Visine failed to be there. The Visine he found was actually Murine. The shoulders of the tiny bottle were coated with grime. It would do. He quickly paid for it and the comb that had appeared on the counter next to it. He wondered if the old man had procured it from his own pocket.

Paying for the purchases, Ned understood something correctly that he'd misinterpreted. There were two black streamers hanging down, one on either side of the MIA flag. Ned had perceived them as something like crepe, something to emphasize the message of the thing. But in fact they were ribbons of tape black with dead flies. Little cylinders of flytrap tape were also counter-top impulse items. He collected his change.

Ned said, "The other thing is the *New York Times*. I'm going to be around here for a few days. I'm staying up the hill . . ." He waited to see if this information brought any reaction from the old man, who pursed his lips and held them pursed for what was arguably an unusually long time.

Ned established that the *Times* came most days, early afternoon, and that the old man would try to save a copy for him, *if* it came. Ned sensed a little coldness now, coming toward him. By asking for the *Times*, Ned had obviously identified himself as a beloathed liberal. This man was concerned with the victims of war and now there was going to be another one. There could be more MIAs for him. Ned was tempted to say something useless.

A large soft mouse-colored old dog, a Labrador, came out from behind the counter and stared at him.

"Could I use your restroom?" Ned asked.

"*Acourse*," the old man said, gesturing unclearly to his right. Ned worked it out. The restroom required a key, which was hanging on a hook at the end of the front counter. Ned reached for the key without realizing that the fine chain running through the hoop of the key also ran down through holes punched in two tire hubs. So there was a certain clangor, of course. Ostensibly this arrangement would be to keep the key from being lost or mislaid, but probably it was also for merriment when the uninitiated grabbed for the key without paying that much attention, as he had done. The restroom was straight back and to the left. He had to pass a vast display of periodicals taking up all the wall space between the counter area and the cross aisle at the back.

He scanned the selection as he passed. Pornorama! he thought.

There was everything. A man could want. *Naughty Neighbors* through *Gent* through *Plumpers* through a startling one, *Whorientals*. Breasts for all. Back near the counter the main newsweeklies formed a thin right-hand margin to this field of pink plenty, and there the *Weekly Standard* predominated, with the last three issues preserved for sale whereas only the current issues of *Time* and *Newsweek* were available. Interestingly, a shower curtain shielded the last quarter of the array of porn. It could be slid aside. The design on the curtain represented the world: through the blue translucencies between the continents, images of handsome male heads and muscular bodies were discernible. Picturesque as all this was, Ned couldn't linger.

A bald, youngish man, very heavy, was seated behind a workbench in a slot punched into the middle of the back wall. Ned crossed in front of him and nodded. The man was repairing a fly rod. As he slumped back in his chair to notice Ned more comfortably, and as his chin sank into his fat throat, his dense, short-cropped yellow beard presented as a sort of Elizabethan ruff along the bottom of his face. Ned thought he had an intelligent look. His arms were lavishly tattooed. He wondered if this could be the fine old man's son. He hoped not, back there all day and probably expected to keep an eye on porn browsers in case they were tempted to take something or whisk something with them into the toilet. Not much of a life for this fellow.

Ned couldn't help but be curious about the tattooed images the young man was displaying, which led straight to a question of etiquette, which was whether it was polite to look at the demons and crosses and daggers decorating his giant arms. On the one hand, they were put there to be noticed, and on the other hand, it would make you look gay. If that bothered you. It was best to treat it like wallpaper.

On the restroom door was a primitive cartoon of a figure that was female on one side, half a skirt, and male on the other, half a top hat.

In the restroom, Ned was quick about everything. He was pointlessly a little proud of the thick, shaggy limb of urine he produced. He rinsed his face with cold water, which was all there was. He decided he looked okay. A little red, white, and blue sticker in the corner of the dull mirror read *Pataki? Ptui!*

6 The bridge was well behind him. It had seemed sturdy enough.

He was almost there. It was a whole hilltop, green, treeless, broadly convex, like the top of a cupcake. It was extensive. His feelings reminded him of what Nina had said about Cézanne's landscapes, that when you see them, you relax. Now he could see the tower, four stories tall, like a stone hatbox. Tower? he thought. Oh, a short one. And roomy-looking. A gravel path branched off from the road and led to the summit, and the tower. He couldn't believe the tower. It was short and it had a parapet notched for archers or shooters, defenders. He couldn't imagine anyone he knew living in such a setting.

He was agitated. But maybe something good could come out of this. This disaster. Their group had been talented. Letters they had written to the *Aegis* in college had always gotten attention. Maybe the others and he could collaborate on a statement against the coming invasion, in their old style. Their letters hadn't all been on the frivolous side. Some hadn't.

7 "Hi, Ma."

"Hi yourself. To what do I owe the honor of thisum."

Nina sighed. It was her mother's way to break off her sentences once she was satisfied that her respondent knew what she was obviously going to say next. Thisums and theums were major building blocks in Ma's discourse. It was odd. Her mother was an odd woman, an odd woman but lovable and she loved her. Her mother didn't trail off as though she were trying to think of the next word. It was just laborsaving. That was how her mother saw it.

"I'm not calling to honor you, I'm calling to give you my whereabouts, such as they are, so you won't worry."

"Yeah, but Nina, what about theum?"

It sounded Greek, but Nina knew what she meant. It was the march, the demonstration, the Convergence. Her mother was a sentimental communist, a very nice old communist living in El Nido, a nice old lady communist apartment complex owned by a nice old rich lady communist widow. It was a family, there. Ned called it Birobidjan after the ghetto province Stalin had tried to corral all the Jews in Russia into, to raise chickens. And in fact in El Nido, they had raised chickens, until the city made them stop. They still had a victory garden. Her mother was a communist and a practicing astrologer. She had slept with John Garfield before she got married. Nina's father had been proud of it and would drop it into conversations.

Nina said, "Where I am is in Kingston New York in a bus station and I'm waiting for a bus to take me to Phoenicia New York. You can only get me on my cell phone, do you understand? And don't worry, the march is going to be enormous. I'll tell you about it. I'll call you when I can."

"Hey, don't hang up Neen! I don't know where you are in New York. And *why* are you in New York?"

"Ma, I wish to God you would get a computer and take a course. I'll pay for it. It's so much better for keeping in touch."

"I have no time. I'm too old."

"Listen to me while I explain where I am. I can't talk to you forever."

"How I wish you could!"

That was her mother being ironical. It was kind of funny.

"Ma, okay, why I'm here. We're supposed to be getting me pregnant. You know. So Ned gets a phone call saying that an old friend died, *died*, not even dying, *dead*. But Ned just ran out and got on a plane and left town. I got this in a message on my answering machine . . ."

The thing was to not keep getting enraged over it.

Ma said, "Oh Nina, was it yourum?"

Sometimes her mother baffled her.

"My *what*?" Nina asked. And then she had it. "Oh my *sharp tongue*, you mean? No, there was no argument, so not my sharp tongue, Ma. What sharp tongue, anyway, you absurd person."

"You have a sharp tongue, Nina."

Her mother never took anything back. Her usual move was to repeat what she'd said but in a tiny voice.

"I didn't get a chance to use my so-called sharp tongue. Now listen. Ned's friends at NYU were—call them a clique—all top students, a clique but serious, this is hard to explain, they were *wits*, too, according to them . . ."

"What do you mean by that? Wits?"

"My very question. Here's an example. They're in with other people having a regular conversation on some subject. And one of Ned's friends inserts a line from a popular song. Right in the middle of things, and with no ado at all Douglas might say to Ned, I don't care what people say Rock and Roll is here to stay, and Ned would say You dig it to the end. And the conversation would just go on. It's just adolescent, Ma."

"I don't get it."

"Anyway, the bandleader of this wonderful group died suddenly and his widow, also known as the most beautiful woman you ever saw, begged Ned to come. So he went. Because she was upset. Everybody from the group was going, so he called me at work and I was out so he left a message *informing me*, Ma. And we're working on a *baby* . . ."

"Nina, you shouldum."

Nina had to control her tone. "*I know. We should adopt. I know your position* . . . So I got on a plane myself. He doesn't know that yet."

"*Who* died?"

"*Ma, I never met him*. He turned out to be rich. And boy was he a whiner. I live in a dying forest, he wrote to Ned. I read that over Ned's shoulder and I felt like saying, Well, move then, you can afford it."

Everything was getting to her. She was looking at a block of identical posters on the bus station wall. Each of them had been neatly defaced with the word *faggot* inscribed in italic marker pen on the forehead of the lead singer of a group called Blue Papa.

Her mother loved Ned. "I love Ned," Ma said. Who doesn't, Nina wanted to say. Ned and her mother had been on the same page in the matter of adoption. She'd had to fight to convince Ned they should have their own child. Christ, what a battle. Finally she had won. What she wanted was Ned's essence, what he was, because he was a lovely man. And face it, she wanted her own essence to go on, too. She was okay, and went well with Ned, as the harsh angel he needed. He should really be a Christian. He was. Be anything, but hold me in your arms, she thought. And then she remembered how much he had laughed last week when she'd said Let's go lie down and call each other honey. She wished sometimes that Christianity was real and that there was a heaven so he could go to heaven, and she would be willing to go to hell for her transgressions. There would be a God and Ned would believe and he would be safe. But he couldn't be a Christian because science was true. And his good friends were all secular. She wasn't religious herself, but for some reason she had pushed Ned to go with her to a couple of Quaker meetings. Society of Friends. She was attracted to what they *called* themselves. But it hadn't worked. It had to do with the silence at the end of the proceedings where people are supposed to speak as the spirit moved them. The spirit had moved Ned to argue with some of the things the spirit had moved other people to say. And that hadn't been appreciated.

"Don't be hard on Ned," Ma said.

"Okay I won't. I'll take it out on his friends."

"Nina, you're going to get pregnant. I know it."

"You're seeing the future again?"

Her mother did think she could see the future, and not only the economic future, with socialism just around the corner. She had intuited that Nina was going to grow up to be a writer because as a tiny child she had liked the smell of freshly sharpened pencils. I'm still waiting to become a writer, she thought. She wouldn't mind that.

"Don't worry about the future, Neen," Ma said.

"Maybe I should see a shrink," Nina said. This was teasing. Her mother was dead set against psychotherapy. In adolescence when Nina had once proposed that she might need to talk to a psychiatrist, Ma had said You don't need a psychiatrist, it's all in your head.

Nina said, "Ma I love you." She thought, His enemy friends can go to hell. Ned was under an illusion. He thought friendships between men were superior. Because—and he had said this!—men didn't want anything back from their true friends, it was all affinity. They didn't, for example, want a baby from them, want them to be a provider for babies, or need them to be on-call confidants. Men are simple, she thought.

"Neen, I love you all the time," Ma said.

"I know you do. I'll call you. These people don't think Ned's important, Ma. They know nothing. They don't know anything about the Fair Trade movement which he's practically a god in. He's helping poor people, the co-operatives . . ."

"Oh honey I know and I lost the catalog you sent me, the coffee catalog."

"I'll send you another one."

"Oh and Nina, I know you have to go, but don't wear buckskin," she said with real anxiety. Ma was referring to a buckskin jacket, fringed, that Nina loved.

This never dies, Nina thought, because with the long black hair that you want me to cut and because I'm so fierce and all, and because looking Sicilian makes me look like a Cherokee in the buckskin. "I don't even own that jacket anymore, Ma," she said, which wasn't true.

"Okay then, that's good. And go easy on the cursing. Remember if you're working with a lot of men you get used to cursing. If these people where you're going live in a castle they might not like it. You told me that his friend lived in a castle. I remember that."

"My bus is here, Ma. Be good."

8 Closer up, the tower looked a little ragged in outline. It was built out of shale flags. There were big windows in every story. It would be hell to heat. It was a major thing, this dark edifice, not a toy, not a tree house. You could put a few families in it.

A running figure, a young man running, flashed twice across Ned's field of vision. The runner was circling the tower. Ned waved vigorously, but the sturdy figure kept running and then failed to reappear. He had been barechested, strangely, given the weather. He had been wearing torn jeans, and on his head, a red bandana, like a pirate or rap singer. He looked tall for fourteen or fifteen, but he had to be Hume, Douglas's boy, who of course would be upset. Probably that was why he was running. I would want my son to be upset if I died, not to mention my daughter, he thought. He was going to be an old father, the kind kids wouldn't prefer, which couldn't be helped. There had been trouble with Hume. Elliot would know, Ned thought. I pray to god it isn't something ugly and predictive of hell. People who had children assuming they were creating future friends were rolling the dice.

The gravel creaked under Ned's boots. The tower's grounds were, Ned now saw, not entirely treeless. A quince tree stood at one corner of Douglas's famous physic garden, which lay behind a gated wire fence. Douglas had alluded to his quince tree more than once. This garden would be where he had raised herbs and other exotic botanicals, presumably for fun.

Someone darkly dressed was squatting next to the

quince tree. This figure's back was toward the tower path, toward Ned. It was his friend Elliot crouching there, smoking. Ned called out and Elliot stood up and, turning, shot his cigarette butt away—furtively, Ned thought. Ned began to trot toward his friend. He was full of feeling. Elliot was a decent man. Ned's eyes felt charged, not ready to let any tears out, but close. From this vantage, Ned could see other buildings set lower on the descending far side of the hill—a vast rustic ranch-style house with smoke rising from a chimney . . . a wide garage, sheds, other structures. Elliot was waving. He shouted, "Ahoy, polloi," an ancient nothing from their student days.

"Ahoy yourself!" Ned said. It was the same Elliot, still thin, professionally tan, now. His dark hair flowed back from not quite the center of his head. He pressed his hair down. He was working up a smile for Ned. It always seemed to take a little effort for Elliot to erect a smile. The group had accepted the responsibility to keep Elliot, with his default permanently resigned expression, cheered up. His long, serious actorly face was unlined. He undoubtedly had the same effect on groups that he'd had in olden times: when he arrived, people would be concerned to place him, figure out who he was, exactly. His height was part of it, of course. Elliot's smile came, and his teeth, Ned noted, were a la mode, that is to say unnaturally white. Nina had perfect godgiven teeth, like her mother. Nina was goodlooking. But compliments made her nervous. The whole subject made her nervous. Maybe because your appearance was so luck of the draw. She turned away questions touching on her looks. Someone had asked her what color she would say her green-brown eyes were, and she had said they were olive drab. Elliot was rich. The two men embraced.

They stood back from one another. Both said, "Ah, man . . ." with feeling.

Elliot was wearing a black leather trench coat worth a fortune. He had the collar up for drama, or possibly protection against wind. There was no wind. A dead calm prevailed. The sound of water draining from the tower's downspouts stood out in the stillness.

Elliot smelled of cigarette smoke. It had been understood among the friends that smokers were the ultimate fools. But the fact was that Elliot had smoked modestly and privately back then. And considerately. It was up to him. Ned doubted that smoking was popular in Douglas's household. In truth, Douglas had been generally intolerable about it. At one point, he had picked up some anti-smoking flyers featuring medical photographs of specimens of leukoplakia, the condition just prior to oral cancer, and had dropped them around in lecture halls and the Commons room. But he hadn't harassed Elliot, or not very much.

They embraced again. Each told the other he was looking great.

Ned was finding it hard to talk normally. He said, "I came right away after you called, this is so fucked. God. Fuck. It's terrible. What happened? What happened that I don't know about?"

Elliot put his arm around Ned's shoulders. He started to say something but then stopped, clearly considering his words, which made Ned a little uneasy. Elliot was a stockbroker and a juris doctor. He had given financial advice to Douglas, and legal advice, too. Ned was prepared for Elliot letting it be felt that he was in a different, or even official, relationship with Douglas's family. This was going to be something more than the usual benign reserve Elliot projected and that intrigued people and made them want to reassure themselves that it wasn't caused by anything they might have done. Ned supposed he had to live with it.

Ned said, "I want to see Douglas."

Elliot shook his head, saying, "No, you can't. They took the body to Kingston." The special relationship had made its appearance.

"Okay, but I want to see him anyway, the physical Douglas."

Elliot nodded rapidly, but signifying understanding and not assent. Ned didn't like it. Ned said, "Have you seen his body?"

"I did, before they took him."

"Well. What's going on? Is there going to be a wake? A funeral service, what?"

"Right now I don't know. I don't know what Iva can take. Douglas is going to be cremated. She's fragile. We're trying to figure this out."

Ned said, "And what about Hume? I just saw him running around back there, around the tower, if that was him, without a shirt on."

Elliot grimaced. He said, "He's upset and he's out of control. To some degree. He has an exceptional arrangement with his parents. He . . . lives outdoors a good deal, and he has just about agreed to home schooling, after a debacle, two of them, with private schools. Douglas built a cabin for him last year. For his independence. He rejected it. He let them do it and then rejected it."

Ned said, "How could this happen?"

Elliot said, "It was a complete accident. He drove the mower too close to the edge of the ravine. That's what happened . . . the autopsy was today."

Ned felt himself shaking, and to quell it, clutched his hands together behind his back and clenched his arms.

"Take that thing off and give it to me," Elliot said, pointing at Ned's rucksack. "Christ, is that the same one you had when we climbed Storm King?"

"It is," Ned answered. "Storm King and the Shawangunks and all of them. It's the only one I've ever had."

"You're loyal to your possessions," Elliot said.

Ned felt a moment of trivial puzzlement. Was Elliot being critical? All it could be was a reference to the fact that he didn't, had never, thrown things away wantonly, while they still had some use in them.

"You're a masochist. Give it to me," Elliot said, guiding Ned toward an ornate door in the base of the tower. Ned held on to his pack. Elliot scrutinized him. "Ned, you need to rest. Come in and rest. We're all here."

Elliot had the door open. Ned was moving reluctantly. It was a concession to go in instead of mobilizing somehow to get to Kingston. He was tired. He murmured something about Kingston but without force. He knew it was in the nature of a reproach to Elliot.

Elliot said, "It makes no sense to go to Kingston. All this is being worked out, Ned."

Elliot patted Ned's shoulder, then pressed him forward, being less patient. Ned said, "All of us are here?"

Ned stopped abruptly, putting Elliot off his stride. Elliot stumbled slightly and began coughing. The coughing went on. Ned was alarmed.

"Why are you coughing?" is what he came out with, surprisingly to himself. Maybe it was anxiety that something was wrong with *this* friend, too, now, someone trying to do his best under stress. He knew what Nina would say. Ned, she would say, you're displacing. Displacement behavior meant getting aggrieved about something that was standing in for something else.

The ground-floor room was sizeable, with a high wood-beam ceiling. The walls were lined with blond wooden filing cabinets, to a height of five feet or so, and above the cabinets ponderous shelving held oversized books and binders. Everything was fitted to the curve of the walls, and all the woodwork was polished to gleaming. The books here seemed to be in the reference category—serials, in bound volumes, quartos, sets. Ned wanted to look more closely at them and also at the items laid out on an oceanic work table pushed against one of the three broad windows. He could see a lightbox on the table, and an array of optical instruments. How long would it take, Ned wondered, to get used to the postcard-quality vistas of placid nature the windows provided? The temptation would be to drift into witless contemplation and then wonder where the time went. And who dusted and cleaned and polished all this? Someone.

A steep and narrow stone stairway ran up to the next story. There were red-orange oriental carpets on the floors. Whether they were top of the line, someone like Claire would know. Immediately he wanted to move past the thought of his ex love and, with a little effort, he did.

Elliot was beckoning impatiently from the stairs.

There was a definite burned smell in the air and a fire-place jammed with ashes, white paper-ash.

Ned said, "Everybody's upstairs, right?"

"Joris is out walking and Gruen is taking a nap. You're all on the third floor. We were up drinking last night."

Ned winced inwardly at that. It was another part of all this that he had missed.

Elliot came down a step or two, reaching toward Ned. He said, "Take your pack off, for Christ's sake, it's a monster. Give it to me."

Ned ignored Elliot's move.

Elliot said, "You're all on the third floor, keep coming. I'll show you your bed. It's dormitory style."

"Where are you sleeping?" Ned asked.

"I'm over in the main house . . . there's a reason."

Ned said, "I need to see Iva, of course, before I do anything, don't I?"

"Not yet," Elliot said. "Not yet."

Elliot kept a forefinger pressed to his lips the whole way up, screwing his head around at intervals like an idiot, to show that he wasn't kidding about silence.

There was a shock for Ned on the third floor. A form completely shrouded in a white blanket encumbered an army cot near the stairhead. Of course it could only be Gruen sleeping in his signature mode, the covers pulled over his head, but for an instant, Ned had thought he was seeing death. Elliot was telling him in a shouted whisper that it was Gruen, and to leave him alone.

Ned went to the cot and bent close to the sleeper, whose rumbling breathing was familiar enough from the deep past. And the wine-tinctured breath sifting up through the blanket was also vintage Gruen, so to speak. Gruen had been the leading drinker in their group.

He felt like lifting the blanket enough to take a look at Gruen. Or rather, he didn't feel like doing that, he felt like not having to wait for everything to happen. How could it be that they hadn't connected physically in twenty years? At around five six, Gruen was the shortest of the friends. And although the hurtful phrase Small but Perfectly Formed hadn't been around in the seventies, if it had been it would have applied to Gruen, then, with his fine Nordic head, his profile cut to go on a coin or medal.

Glancing around, Ned decided that sleeping there would be fine, if it couldn't be avoided. Views left and right—calm prospects, no crags, just the matte grandeur of tracts of trees sweeping up to plucked-looking ridgelines, marred, if that was the word, here and there by isolate slumping-limbed firs resembling incorrect ideograms. Scenery is probably good for your blood pressure, he thought. Set into the wall back of the stairhead was a sort of booth whose door was ajar. It was a half-bath, rosily lit. So there was everything.

A pair of lustrous black cowboy boots stood at the foot of Gruen's cot. He wore boots for the obvious reason, and in fact Ned had been the one to encourage him not to be embarrassed about making the transition from regular shoes if it made him more comfortable, which it had.

The bare cot with the block of folded bedclothes on it was going to be his. He was next to Joris, whose cot was neatly made up. Joris had always been tidy, which reminded Ned of an incident: their group in the village, strolling down Mercer Street, Douglas saluting some sanitation men at work there and calling out the phrase NEW YORK'S TIDI-EST, which the men hadn't liked, and had resulted in filth of some kind finding its way onto Douglas's new shoes. Ned wouldn't mind discussing the subject of just how funny most of their japes had been.

Lined up across Joris's pillow were a shaving kit, a cordless LED reading light, and a new hardcover copy of *The Twilight of American Culture*, by Morris Berman. It was a luxury, buying books new, but somebody had to do it, and if Joris could afford it, good for him.

Ned stowed his things under the cot meant for him. He wanted Joris to appear, and Gruen to wake the fuck up. Elliot was talking furtively on his cell phone, again. He wanted to go up to the next level, to Douglas's study. He wanted to see Douglas's sanctum. He didn't need permission. This sleeping room was uninteresting. It was storage. Around the periphery were tables loaded with books and periodicals. There were more books piled under tables. There was another vast oriental rug underfoot. He mounted to the next level while Elliot continued in conversation.

Ned was in distress. It was all right because it was going to go away. He was sitting in Douglas's desk chair, a heavy throne-like baronial thing that could roll smoothly to any point along the wooden desk ledge that encircled the room, except for two interruptions, one for a fireplace and one for the circular iron stairway to the tower roof, where Ned wanted to go next. He might feel better up there, if only because it would get him out of this ultimate venue for a person to think and work in, ever. Douglas's study was not only esthetically elevating, it was consummately equipped, the essential tools distributed intelligently around the scene. He was seated in front of the computer-scanner-printer complex, next to the phone-fax setup, and a short slide away from an imposing stereo layout. There was an intercom microphone at hand and next to it the speaker that went with it. The lighting was mostly green-shaded bankers' lamps, with a few tensors included for variety. Where Douglas had found a completely round Persian rug was a question. Ned's feet encountered a couple of ten-pound dumbbells under the desk. Douglas had once announced his intention to die thin as a curate. They had all been thin, then, Gruen less so. There were no photographs of Douglas on display. In fact the only images in the little selection on the wall to the right of the desk were of Douglas's boy Hume. They were all early childhood pictures.

Everything was a fount of sadness. This perfect workplace sitting empty, abandoned by the one it was perfect for, abandoned abruptly years too soon. There was only one photograph that wasn't of Hume as a small child. The disparate one was a framed tear-out from an ancient tabloid showing Sophia Loren shooting a disconcerted sidelong glance at her dinner partner Jayne Mansfield's cleavage. That was Douglas. Ned didn't like it that Iva wasn't represented, nor anyone other than Hume who was related to him in any way. The friends had been a presentable group, overall. Douglas had taken the position that his success with women at NYU was a mystery to him. Nina, studying one of the few photos Ned possessed from their college days, had suggested that Douglas's success had been attributable to a brooding manner and his permanent five o'clock shadow, the political prisoner look.

Ned heard his name being spoken below. He wanted to get out on the tower roof before he went downstairs.

He knew he was looking at something salient but not seeing it. At the center of the miscellany of books lining the back edge of the section of desk right in front of him was Douglas's Oxford UP paperback copy of Boswell's *Life of Samuel Johnson*. Douglas had been an absolute Johnsonomane. And in a fax communication years ago, he'd claimed that he'd gotten so much pleasure out of reading *The Life* that he'd stopped and placed a bookmark at page 847 so that he would have finishing the book in pleasant increments to look forward to. And here it was. Ned pulled the book from the shelf. It was bookmarked at page 847. He slipped the book into his rucksack. Douglas had related powerfully to Samuel Johnson somehow. All the friends had been hectored to read the damned thing. It was great, of course.

The stereo's power light was on. Impulsively, he pressed the open/close button and removed the CD the tray delivered. This would have been one of the last things Douglas had listened to. It was Vivaldi's Concerto for Guitar in D Major played by the Wiener Soloisten. He found the jewel case, put the CD away in it, and slid the case into his pocket.

Out on the roof, the wind was raw and lurching. Dark was coming fast. There was a ludicrous parapet around the roof with embrasures useful only for archers who were toddlers. The pebbled surface of the roof was convex, for drainage. Ned didn't want to pitch over the side. He concentrated on his footing. A telescope on a tripod was wrapped in black plastic sheeting bound tightly with long twist ties. Probably he should take it inside. Out of the way, a child's wooden chair lay on its side, bleached, coming apart, obviously abandoned years ago.

Gruen was calling to him.

"Don't come up," Ned said. "There's nothing here."

Gruen looked lost standing beside his cot, wrapped in blankets, using a bath towel for a hood. He had a cold, he was saying, with difficulty. He shook a Kleenex at Ned as a warning sign of his condition.

"I don't care," Ned said, and embraced him. Both of them wept briefly. Elliot had gone into hiding in the main house. Joris was still wherever he was.

It was maudlin, for a time. Ned let himself go. Gruen had a sore throat and kept saying he had to stop talking. But they went on. Gruen pulled his towel down for use as a scarf. Ned could see his face clearly then. His hair was thinner, and was auburn, to Ned's surprise. Gruen had gained weight. His face was still youthful, though, somehow. Gruen owned an agency dedicated to creating public service announcements for television. He was under the impression that Ned was still living with Claire, Douglas's Claire of the old days. Ned had to explain that he and Claire hadn't been together for five years, and that he would tell the whole long story when Joris got there. He didn't want to have to repeat it. He was married to Nina and he had never been married to Claire. He underlined that. Both men expressed guilt for not staying in better touch with one another, and with Douglas. In different ways, they were repeating disbelievingly that the founder of their group, their friendship, was suddenly dead, and here they were, camped out in the pretty stupefying domain he had left behind. Gruen had no children. He wondered if Claire had been informed about Douglas's death and Ned said she would see it in the papers, probably already had. He wanted to shake the shadow of Claire off them, away. They wondered together what was going to happen to Iva now. Gruen said that Douglas's son, according to his latest understanding, lived in the woods, strangely enough. There was going to be a ceremony. And press was coming, was already coming, and Elliot was in charge, giving orders. Gruen said that Douglas had been more famous in Europe than they had known.

Abruptly, Gruen sat down. He said something about steam, and tea. Ned tried to think of what he could do. Upstairs in the study there had been a niche with a minikitchen built into it—no stove, but a midget microwave oven. And he had noticed a box of Earl Grey in the vicinity. He would take care of it in a minute.

Gruen was fishing around in his wrappings. He said, "I brought this," handing Ned a milky Polaroid photograph. Ned studied it. There they were, their group circa 1974 when they'd lived together off campus on the Lower East Side at 71 Second Avenue. He remembered the super taking this picture, organizing them in the widest part of their railroad apartment, the dining ell. There they were, sitting in disparate kitchen chairs, facing the future. Ned had worn his hair longer, then: the wavy front rose up in a way that now reminded him of bleachers. Douglas was the only one presenting in profile, very Apollonian, except for his unusually prominent Adam's apple. A spatula was protruding from the breast pocket of Douglas's tweed jacket, for no reason. It was not meant to suggest that Douglas was connected to any cooking duties. Joris had his hands on his knees and was leaning forward in a crouch, scowling balefully. Gruen was staring into the bowl of a Meerschaum pipe, seemingly perplexed, being a clown. There was at least one other dumb group shot, as he recalled. In it, Douglas, in bathing trunks, was aiming a hand mirror at his navel and Elliot was smirking into the inside pages of a gag *New York Times* they had had printed up at a novelty shop, whose headline was, in forty-eight-point type, SEA GIVES UP ITS DEAD. What dumb jape he himself had been engaged in for the camera he didn't remember. The group portrait in his hand would, in the ultimate dimness, be all there was of the five of them as an organism.

Gruen told Ned he could have the photo. Ned didn't want it.

"You keep it," Ned said to Gruen, who shook his head. Ned put the photo in the pocket containing the Vivaldi CD.

Not going over to present himself to Iva at the main house was beginning to seem idiotic. And he hadn't seen Hume, except fleetingly, if in fact that had been Hume. True, he was deferring to the strong, what? Requests or instructions of an old friend. He could put it off a little longer, he guessed, without seeming rude. He was going to try Nina again. And when Joris turned up, they would go over together, unless Joris could provide a good reason to obey Elliot. Ned was upset with Elliot.

Gruen was lying down again, again shrouded to the top of his head. Ned decided to erect a card table at a considerate distance from Gruen. Ned had brought him a cup of tea. He retrieved the empty cup from inside the blanket cave Gruen was keeping himself in. Nina continued to not answer.

Ned opened up four folding chairs and placed them around the card table. Earlier, he had located the thermostat. He was satisfied that the baseboard heating strip was functioning. His cardigan would be adequate for warmth. He had laid out his petitions and some ancillary paperwork on the table. For light, there was a floor lamp and a ruby-red pillar candle on a dinner plate. Joris would have book matches or a lighter. So would Elliot, but where was he when you needed him?

He settled himself. Company! he thought. He was hearing definite sounds of arrival, followed by sounds of ascent.

Joris looked joyful, seeing Ned. He sprang into the room from the top step and ran over to Ned and stood there with his arms spread wide, gesturing with his hands for Ned to stand up and endure what would be a crushing hug. So Ned did, full of happiness himself. Joris was the least changed. Or maybe they were in a tie. Joris had all his hair, solidly gray, dense as ever, cropped short. He and Ned were the same height, but Joris was powerfully built. He had heavy brows, a hard face generally. He had a low blink rate that Douglas had observed and proved to him. He did project a kind of Teutonic severity, which had led to Douglas referring to him *just once* as the Hun. His background was Latvian.

Joris ducked into the half-bath and closed the door. They had yet to get to the death that brought them all there. Ned waited. Joris was the smartest of them. He had gone from mathematics to maritime law, he had had the darkest worldview available then. Joris came out of the half-bath. Somewhere he had found a bottle of Evian water and two tumblers, which he brought to the table. "It's warm," he said, indicating the bottled water.

"That doesn't matter," Ned said.

"Should we talk quietly?" Joris asked, pointing his chin at Gruen.

"I'm awake," Gruen said.

"Then you should get up," Joris said.

"I'll get up for dinner."

Joris said something unfathomable to Ned. It was definitely a word. He had said it in his throat. Joris had been raised speaking Latvian at home and English at school. His mother had gone deaf when he was young. For Joris, speaking English seemed a little effortful. Often he gave the impression he was concentrating what he needed to say into pellets, which he delivered after longish intervals. Wait, no, it wasn't his mother who had gone deaf, it was his father. He'd gone deaf working in the quarry he owned. He was like the king of a rainy country: own a veritable gold mine of a quarry, work it, work in it, get prosperous, go deaf.

Ned and Joris gripped hands across the table, elbows on the tabletop, as though they were going to arm-wrestle. "I concede," Ned said. It was the way many discussions between them had ended.

"So, you bastard, you came. Hello," Joris said.

They talked sadly about the freakishness and unfairness of Douglas's fate. All of them were going to be saying the same things over and over to one another. Douglas had been a man attentive to what he ate, hyperattentive. He had taken care of himself.

Closing the topic for the moment, Ned said, "The group is finished."

"No," Joris said, in a voice loud enough to cause Gruen to thrust his head back into the room. "It was finished *long ago*."

"What?" Gruen asked.

Ned said, "He doesn't mean dead from the beginning." He looked at Joris, who hesitated but finally said what Ned wanted to hear, "No, nono."

"What were we, nineteen seventy-four to nineteen seventy-eight, the five of us?" Ned asked generally.

Joris closed his eyes. He was considering.

Ned had his own private image of that time. He saw himself looking back, down a very long road, at night, and seeing dimly lighted establishments spaced along the road—but at one point, far back, a gathering of bright lights something like an arcade or a carnival, red and gold lights and shreds of music coming from that location only. It was cheap.

"Look at me, I'm emotional," Joris said. He was going to say more. Ned knew it was a sign that Joris was ready to give his finished opinion when he took his glasses out of his shirt pocket and laid them down in front of him, as he was doing.

Joris said, "What we were . . . well, I could quote from when we discussed this on the phone a few years ago: I said we were a cult, but not exactly a cult, a cult of friendship. We got the whole idea of it from Douglas. Without it, we would have made ordinary connections like everybody else does passing through college and not noticed anything particular about that. And some of us might not have made any connections at all. I am not naming names . . ."

Ned knew enough about Joris's life to provide a base of real sympathy. They had been in contact through letters, and then email, and very rarely by phone, through the years. Joris's marriage had produced twin boys, now grown, both in pre-med, one at the University of Hawaii, one at a dubious school in the Caribbean. Joris was divorced. He had divorced and had never remarried for what had always seemed to Ned a singular reason. He had described himself as a married-woman fetishist, that is, a fetishist for married women except the one he was married to. And he realized it was going to ruin any marriage he undertook the same way it had wrecked the first one. Helen was the name of his first wife. Joris had said that maritime law was a perfect field for him because absolute cynicism was the best Weltanschauung to have if you were in it, because the field was strewn with pirates and crooks.

Gruen was up. He was in the broom closet aka bathroom, running water, and repeatedly blowing his nose.

Joris said, "Man you know there's a toilet on every floor, don't you? And a shower in the first-floor one. Not very big, though."

Gruen rejoined them. God he was really plump.

"I would like to add something," Gruen said, acting stately. "We were *friends* . . ."

"I am coming to that," Joris said, his voice raised.

Gruen got out of his bathrobe and gathered up his clothes. Then, standing facing out one of the great windows, dressed himself. Blasts of rain struck the glass. It was turning black, out.

For sex, Joris went to prostitutes. There were prostitutes of every caliber in Manhattan, and Joris had the money. This had gone on for years, was still going on, no doubt. Joris claimed he had never gotten an STD. And going to whores had given him a *Decameron* of stories. A drawback was that going to prostitutes meant having to use condoms all the time. Joris rarely saw his sons.

Joris said, "We tried as hard to be friends as anyone. And we *were* good friends. And what else. We were big moviegoers, cineastes, even, always at the Thalia or the Eighth Street. For a while we were a hiking club. We climbed Storm King. We hiked and then we stopped hiking. The girlfriends took over but we kept on the best we could. We carried books up to the tops of mountains and sat there and read them for forty-five minutes. In the dorm and also on Second Avenue we would sit and listen to good music, records, nobody allowed to speak. You could put it this way, we were a very strict book club run by Douglas. We made jokes. You could say that most of the time we carried out Douglas's jokes. And here is the thing, my men. Nothing was funny that we did. Nothing. Almost. Stop objecting until you sit down with us, you there." He meant Gruen.

Over his shoulder, Gruen said, "I'd like to point out that we were also dean's list, all of us. And that we were getting grades fucking nicely. Everybody moved on, everybody did well."

Joris groaned theatrically. "I'm almost through. And you're right about that. There was something else we were getting at being . . ."

Ned said, "Molecular socialism."

The other two knew what he meant. It was embarrassing to recall how seriously he had taken the whole thing, the world remade, friendship at the core of everything.

Gruen faced them in his dinnerwear, a heavy Irish white cable knit sweater, wide-leg khaki pants, loafers.

"Where are your socks?" Ned asked him.

"Every pair is wet since I got here."

Ned went to his rucksack to dig out a pair to lend to Gruen.

Gruen looked flushed. He said, "Also don't forget it wasn't boring, the whole time, mostly. In the subway or waiting around for anything, we had games, like the Hollywood stars gave a picnic and Bogart brought the yogurt, you remember."

Yes, Ned thought, plenty of word games: a bouncer was an excort and graffiti artists were ulterior decorators and Pinot Noir meant don't urinate at night.

Joris was in the half-bath in the room they were sharing so Ned went upstairs to find the facility in Douglas's studio. What looked like a narrow bookcase was the door to the micro-bath. It was at the end of the circle of desks by the stairs. It was nice inside. He sat down on the toilet. Taped to the door in front of him at eye level was an eight-by-ten reproduction of a Paul Klee painting, which amounted to a grid of dots of different colors, at the bottom left paling to dimness and then to nothing. It had been torn out of a bound volume by somebody. The painting's title was DAS GANZE IST DÄMMERNED/THE WHOLE IS DIMMING.

Lo, potpourri in a tray on the toilet tank, a mass of rose petals and other petals. This was Douglas's workplace bathroom. It was pretty feminine. Ned washed his hands and fingered the hand towels, delicate things. Women who love us, he thought, do things for us in ways they think we'll love.

They were waiting.

We were so cineastic, Ned thought, but he rarely went to the movies now. Douglas had been serious about Film, writing tart notes to the *Village Voice* correcting the views of their house movie critic Andrew Sarris. And each of the friends had been assigned a physical double from the world of movies: Douglas's had been Leslie Howard, Joris's had been John Garfield, Elliot's had been an all purpose B-movie villain named John Ireland, and Gruen's double had been the athlete whose name he couldn't think of who played Flash Gordon in Saturday serials. And he himself had been informed that he was the double of the wavy-haired leading man Marx Brother Zeppo, until he'd exploded at Douglas over the stupidity of it. He remained without a double. Flash Gordon had been Buster Crabbe.

Ned asked Joris if he went to the movies much.

"No. Not much. I don't know. I don't enjoy the experience."

An intercom said to come to dinner. The effect was institutional.

Everybody got up. Gruen asked them how he looked. The truth was that he looked like a model for Big Man clothing, a handsome fat man. Joris answered by nodding vigorously and Ned did the same.

They descended to leave.

Rain blew in as they opened the tower door. Douglas inserting the word *egad* into every answer he gave in Cohen's Medicis class had been funny to him.

They went single file into the night, Joris leading.

9 Even in the dark the disconcerting bulk and reach of the main house came through. The place was lit to the gills—the whole interior flushed with light, walkway fixtures blazing, shrubbery spotlit. And Ned had been told that

there was more to the edifice than at first met the eye, e.g., three lower levels were built onto the back of the house, down the far side of the hill. Joris was plying the front-door knocker, a masterpiece of the smithy's art.

Ned tapped Gruen's shoulder. He said, "Hey remember the plan to buy an old manse in some rundown neighborhood near a good university and all of us retiring there together? Get a handyman special and work on it?" The idea had been to die together one by one as friends.

No one was answering the door.

Gruen said, "How I got along so well with Douglas was this. I said everything he said was great. I never said anything worse than Food for Thought."

Ned said, "Probably a good idea, about the insights he kept sending."

Gruen said, "Some of it was interesting. He had his cosmological scenarios. But I lied to him about following the syllabus. That was too much. I got hold of some of the titles, though, physically, thinking . . . someday, okay. He knew I wouldn't read everything. *Reflections on the Causes of Human Misery* I didn't finish. And it was short, an essay."

"Ah, Barrington Moore," Ned said.

"Barrington Moore. Who wrote a lot. Douglas loved him."

The door opened and they all went in.

They seemed to be progressing from one waiting area to another. They had taken their coats off. They were in an annex off the front hall and they were still waiting.

There was ambient music. It was Dvořák. Ned said, "Douglas hated background music."

Elliot appeared but only long enough to say he'd be right back. They were left to study the woodwork. It was like being inside a large armoire with soft lighting.

Since it was a sin to waste time, Ned decided to use the moment to agitate for the Convergence. He took a folded petition and a Bic pen from the inside pocket of his jacket. Joris unfolded the petition, glanced at the heading, refolded it almost immediately and handed it back to Ned. His expression was apologetic.

Ned was startled. He assumed Joris had misunderstood what he'd given him.

Ned said, "It's for Senate Foreign Relations. Next week the resolution authorizing force goes up. I'll get a few more signatures around here and overnight it with the others I have on Monday."

Joris shook his head. He made a negative sound. Ned stared at Joris. Gruen, not current in the stage their discourse had reached, said, "Another thing I never read was the sort-of-manifesto he wrote. It was against war. *Strike When the Gorgon Blinks!* It was a little long. I feel bad about it."

"I never saw it," Ned said, "so how long ago was this?"

"I don't know. Wait, I think Grenada was in it."

Ned turned to Joris. "They're going to do it. Unless we—"

Joris cut him off. "I don't care. Let them."

Ned felt a pain inside as much like acute indigestion as anything else. It wasn't indigestion and he was feeling cold.

"I don't believe you," Ned said.

"Believe me," Joris answered, as Elliot rejoined them, beckoning.

. . .

The interior of the manse was a poem to money and wood-craft. What had it been like for Douglas to conduct his life in perfect hand-carved settings. They were being led to the kitchen. He would like to have a name for the style of the rooms when he gave Nina his account of the trip. Rustic modern might do it. I hate money, he thought, which is adolescent of me. Sometime after college, Douglas had fallen into a huge bequest. Had he known it was on the horizon when they were egalitarians together at NYU? Nothing had been said.

They entered the kitchen, a wonder of its own, like a layout for some glossy culinary-supply catalog. On the subject of money again, if he was correct it was Douglas who'd observed that you never had the full attention of someone with a large stock portfolio while the market was open.

There was Iva, and Iva was a splendid-looking woman. She was standing at the far end of the kitchen island, weeping but not sobbing, keeping on with some cooking project. They drew around her. Iva was slicing the poles off many small onions. She seemed incapable of saying more than Thank you, in a murmur, saying it over and over. Bread was baking. There was a pan of fresh biscuits on a side counter. The woman was evidently in a cooking mania. There were platters of sliced meat set out, warm meat, he gathered, because the plastic film covering the platters was fogged.

She embraced each of them. To Ned, she felt overheated. He thought, You blend an undertone of perspiration with a good perfume and it's erotic. The kitchen was very hot.

Now she was chopping cilantro. Hell she was theatrically beautiful. She had a Tartar face, almost, a face from the image-world of vintage Russian movies or operettas like *The Merry Widow*. Her skin was tended-looking. Her shaped eyebrows were art. She had suave hair the color of brass. It was pulled straight back and a single heavy braid fell over her shoulder. She was wearing a too-big long-sleeved white shirt with a mandarin collar. About her sturdy bosom the less said the better. She was wearing black elf pants. He didn't know any other name for them. She was forty-three. Nina was six years younger. Iva was barefoot. She was solid. Nina would say she could stand to lose three or four pounds. *Naughty Marietta* was another light opera.

That was it for the cilantro. She had expertise. She had moved on to opening jars of pimentos and artichoke hearts. She said, with difficulty, "I know you are all hungry." Everybody nodded vigorously to vindicate her berserk industry. It was funny to Ned that she still sounded so German after living in America as long as she had. Of course, she was Czech, but Czechoslovakia had been part of the greater German culture-zone, so possibly she sounded Czech, in fact. How would *he* know?

The grouping in the room was odd. Elliot was standing apart, superintending. The others had all been able to make some kind of personal condolences to Iva, and Ned hadn't. Now Elliot seemed to be nudging the group prematurely toward the dining room.

Ned touched Iva's arm. He said, "I loved Douglas. He was my friend and I loved him."

He'd had no intention of soliciting a second embrace. But possibly he had moved too abruptly, judging by her reaction, a vehement gesture that utterly baffled him. She seemed to be pointing at her armpits.

Elliot interpreted the moment for him in low, tight words, to the effect that she felt she hadn't had time to clean up properly. It was odd. She had embraced everybody freely a minute earlier. "She's fragile," Elliot said.

Iva said, "Tomorrow we can sit."

"Sure," Ned said.

"She was in Kingston seeing the body today. She's exhausted," Elliot said.

She undid two or three shirt buttons, pulled the front of her shirt forward and shook it. More tears came, and tears and perspiration seemed to be uniting in a yoke around her throat.

Ned wanted to say something about Hume, or rather *to* Hume. The boy's father was dead. Ned wanted to tell Hume he had loved his father. Then he would have said it to both of the survivors and he would be easier waiting for the next developments. "Is Hume here?" he asked, keeping any urgency out of his voice.

Iva seemed to be trying to formulate something to say. The effort failed. Elliot was beside her, consulting, and then almost immediately leading her away. He pushed his palms toward the friends, briefly, to enjoin patience. It was confusing. Elliot said something about eating in the kitchen as he left. There were stools that could be pulled up to the island.

"Hume is here," Joris said, pointing to a doorway.

Iva was gone. Raised voices were coming from somewhere else in the house.

"My boy Hume! Come over!" Joris said. He was being cordial but his voice was too loud.

Standing half in shadow in a doorway in the back wall of the kitchen was the person Ned had glimpsed earlier, the running person.

The boy was strongly built and seemed tall for his age

of fourteen or fifteen. He was ruddy. He wore his hair in a double Mohawk, something new to Ned. He was dressed in leather, black pants or chaps and a vest. There was a symbol hanging around his neck, metal, not a cross, large. He stepped out of sight. Joris dashed after him. He returned quickly, defeated. Elliot came into the room. He looked pink. Ned thought, Dislocation everywhere. Gruen had placed stools around the island and was already furling back the plastic wrap on one of the meat platters.

Let's get in a circle and wring each other's hands, Ned thought.

"I have to return phone calls," Elliot said, but sat down and began pushing platters around.

Gruen surveyed the collation and said, "There are scones here someplace."

Where had Hume gone? Joris was off looking for him again somewhere in the bowels of the woodbutcher's palace, as Douglas had referred to his house. Again Joris was back. Gruen had decanted pan drippings into a teacup. Now he was rolling slices of veal into tubes and carefully making them au jus before each bite.

Elliot said to all of them, "I know we haven't had much time to talk, and I apologize. Tomorrow we will. Right now I have the phones turned off, but I have to put the system back on. I have a bunch of saved calls I have to answer. It's been crazy here. Press is coming, a man named Fusco, Dominique Fusco, might show up tonight. We might see some police around. It has nothing to do with any of you, of course. Loose ends is all. And I'm trying to get a doctor to come in for Iva. But you should eat."

Joris was at the massive refrigerator. Opening both doors wide, he said, "Looking for the butter."

Elliot rose and said sharply, "Don't touch anything in there. She doesn't like it . . . because, ah, because everything's arranged. Everything you need is on the counter."

Joris said nothing. The exaggerated slowness with which he closed the refrigerator doors was his reply.

Ned said, "What about Hume? Can we do something? Shouldn't he eat?"

Elliot said, "He's so upset now it's hard to talk to him. He has a room here and he, well, he has his own place outside, too, his cabin. And he also stays up in the woods in good weather, in a, well, a yurt. But not in weather like this, usually. Have to be careful with him."

"Elliot, you look bad," Ned said.

"She can't sleep. I'm staying over here. Maybe she'll sleep tonight."

Ned said, "You need to come over and talk to us."

"I know. I want to. Maybe tonight, if I can't sleep, if it's okay and you're all still awake or if it's okay if I wake you up if I come over late." Elliot was showing anxiety, which wasn't like him. He had suddenly decided to load crackers with brie, like a hostess, but when he saw that he had overproduced, he stopped.

Joris was eating standing up. The meal array was topheavy with meats—Black Forest ham and Virginia ham, both, along with the roast veal and a selection of Italian charcuterie. Joris was addressing a clod of rice salad. There was pickled okra. There were sliced heirloom tomatoes the color of raw liver. There was nothing green. The okra was khaki-colored. There was wine, red and white, in carafes. Joris discovered a stick of butter thawing on a saucer under a napkin.

A timer rang and Elliot leapt to the oven and frantically

extracted a large loaf, barehanded, which he deposited in the empty sink. "I got it, it's okay," he shouted.

Elliot said, "Really, I have to go."

Ned said, "If you can, come on over."

Gruen wanted some of the fresh, hot bread, so there was a brief interval of comedy as he mangled the loaf in tearing away his portion of it, leaving a crushed rump for the others. It came back to Ned that Gruen had always inordinately loved the interior of freshly baked French or Italian bread.

Ned and Joris looked at each other with the same intent, to register forgiveness for their old friend Gruen. They loved the man. They were being reminded of it. He had been the most hapless and the most naked about showing he was honored to be part of the group. And Gruen had always been weak in the presence of good eats. Ned thought, We are what we were, but *more so* under stress, in extremis, like now. Death was fucking with the bonny boys of 71 Second Avenue. And they were dealing from *strength*, with death. Everybody had life insurance. A metal device wasn't dropping screaming out of the sky to destroy them and their families forever. There was a Greek word for the category of promising people who met untimely deaths. One of his professors had used the word when he'd announced the death of a young colleague, weeping. He had called them the *aoroi*.

They should probably clean up the kitchen before they left for the tower. There was plenty of help associated with the place, but still.

He didn't feel like it.

10 It was medievally cold in the tower. They were all wearing their day clothes in bed. A leg had come off the card table they had been using previously. A staff member, an older man, had wrestled a replacement table up the stairs. This table was pine, and its surface featured black rays left by untended cigarettes, ringmarks in the original veneer, all preserved under laminate. The ghosts of careless drinking days clung to the table, had been invited to cling. Ned wondered if Douglas had acquired the table from one of their haunts in the Village, like the Cedar. There was a battery-powered hurricane lamp on the table, also courtesy of the older man. Any one of them could reach it easily without getting up when it was time to put out the lights.

Ned's spirits were low. Nina was still refusing to answer his calls. Gruen had announced that he was through talking for the night. That was fine.

Joris said, "I'll tell you what I don't want to talk about anymore: what I think about all the comedy we kept trying to do. What I think about it is . . . it was about having fun and the truth is we felt a bit superior, you know."

Ned said, "Vietnam was over and none of us had had to go to Canada. No we felt like we could play around. So we did dada, I suppose, warmed over. I was a raw youth. I thought dada meant Salvador Dalí. I didn't know anything. And did you know by the way that Douglas did a paper on dada for Mouvement des Idées? He actually studied it."

"So enough about that," Joris said.

"So okay, then I want to talk about Iraq. I want all of us to sign my petition," Ned said.

Joris sighed. He said, "Okay, let's get down to preliminaries."

Before Ned could begin, Joris said, "You can't stop mass stupidity. We keep having wars. They never make sense. One thing might help. Somebody beats the shit out of us worse than Vietnam did. If the streets were so full of cripples it fucked up traffic possibly the government would notice."

"Be serious."

"I am. Listen, when there was conscription there was a chance you could stop them. But they figured that out. Now it's mercenaries and the unemployed, a lot of them. And women who want to get in on it. War is like the stock market. I know about this. People spend their whole lives showing what the crooks are doing every day in the market and nobody pays attention, and I will tell you this, you can spend your life on it, and you can die, and the next day the market is doing the same thing. Maybe you've seen some of my letters to the *Financial Times*."

"But Joris. Let me tell you this. It's different, this protest. It's going to be in every country, practically. And *I* know about this. I know what's coming in Europe. It's more like the Resistance. Wait until you see the marches. We can stop it this time."

"Okayokay."

"Will you sign, then? We all have to sign."

Joris said nothing.

Ned said, "Just think about it, and don't forget that every war is men trying to kill each other who have nothing against each other . . ."

Joris cut in, his voice hot. "Douglas said one true thing.

He said War is the continuation of business as usual by any means necessary. So let's stop there."

"Okay then, later. I'm not through."

"Oh Jesus how well do I know."

They yawned synchronously. Ned had another subject, not as important but still important, he wanted to take up with Joris. He wanted to tell the story of Claire, and what had happened on that front. He had to do it right and not put Claire down. Gruen knew most of the Claire saga. He wanted to tell Joris about Nina, too, but not until Gruen could be part of the audience. And he was reluctant to go into the pregnancy question. It might not work. It was Joris who had said in the old days that babies were the only form in which we can love mankind. Now he had two grown sons.

Ned said, "Briefly about Claire . . ." Douglas's stellar fiancée manquée Claire had turned up in Berkeley five years after graduating from NYU after Douglas had dumped her over something still unknown. Ned was managing the Pacific Cooperative Market on Telegraph Avenue when he saw her again, for the first time. She was brought to him in his office for shoplifting a couple of packets of saffron. She was a wraith, then. The breakup with Douglas had been catastrophic. She was at Cal doing graduate work in musicology and then it had happened and they had lived together for the next seven years. They'd had different reasons for not wanting to have children, hers temperamental and his, big surprise, ideological. Post Claire, with Nina, he wanted children, or a child. The idea had been to start an adoption process after they had gone through whatever the fertility clinic proposed. She was willing to adopt.

"Talk about Claire," Joris said.

Ned said, "The situation was that Douglas dropped Claire and she was in bad shape when she came to Cal and we found each other. And we stayed together for a few years and I heard from Douglas through the usual group communiqués, but he never said a word about Claire. And I felt like I didn't have any reason to bring it up either. So anyway, I finished my master's on the decline and fall of the ejido collective in Mexico. I liked Mexico but I couldn't stand to be there for long. I couldn't see teaching. So I worked with the co-ops in the Bay Area. And then got into Fair Trade. Which I do now. Claire traveled a lot. She was in a recorder consort the whole time. She got tenure at Mills College. She traveled both to perform and teach. Anyway, she traveled for her business and I traveled for mine."

"I like what you do for a living," Joris said.

"I like it too." Ned felt like saying thanks. "About Claire, seven years seems like a long time. But the substance of living together kept getting thinner. She was so beautiful that I never got over that she was mine, even if what I had was really a shrinking percentage of her. Go to a party and people would still stop talking when she came into the room and shift around so they could keep looking in her direction."

All the friends had had serious girlfriends at college, at one time or another. And Claire's liaison with Douglas had been almost a marriage. They had been aiming, all of them, at the sublime of work, the sublime of love, the sublime of deeply comprehending the world. It had been essential not to be a fool in any of those departments. And it had looked like Douglas had landed the love-sublime ahead of everybody, with Claire.

Ned went on, "Then she and I had run our course. And since Claire I've been with Nina. Married for the last three years." He paused. "So now Claire lives with a woman in Sonoma County. Her partner is an art photographer, and also commercial. She does high fashion, local celebrities, and so on. Her work is collected. Museums buy her stuff. In fact she did a gallery show with lots of nude studies of Claire in it. We got an invitation. I didn't go. Nina went."

Joris grimaced. He said, "We all loved Claire. She must be bi. That's stupid, what else would she be? And . . . financially. I hope you don't mind if I ask. How did it come out?"

"Fine. We never married. She always earned. And her partner is rich."

Ned thought, The impulse is to tell the story of your life to a friend, so you know what the story is . . . Nina knows a lot . . . but you edit. She's sensitive.

He felt tired. He hoped that was enough to say. Joris said something to himself. Then there was silence.

They brought up the subject of Hume at the same time. Ned let Joris go first. "I don't know what Douglas was thinking, with this boy. He always wanted him to be a joker, like he wanted us to be the Marx Brothers. Why? When Hume was little, Douglas got him the *Johnson Smith Catalog* and every birthday said to him to spend a hundred dollars, two hundred, whatever he liked . . . the boy is very wild. But hell, nothing we can do that I can think of. He has a mother . . . tomorrow we can talk about your wife, maybe."

"After breakfast," Ned said.

It was all right. Ned turned the lantern off. He would lower himself into sleep down a ladder of thoughts of Nina, his honey monkey. He would imagine he was hearing somebody singing "Ombra mai fu." He liked opera, thanks to Nina and not the patrician Claire, he might add. He believed Nina liked opera and Kurosawa movies for the same reason, they were *all out*. Nina was small but not really petite, and very brunette, next to Claire, whose yellow hair was so fine it looked luminous. Claire treated her breasts like blisters, you had to be so gentle. But Nina would play with you, and she might say, Okay, you can feel me up, but only one breast, take your pick. Yes, and the time Claire had stared coldly at him when he'd cupped her breast and pushed her nipple with his thumb-tip and asked Is the missus home? Terrible violation. Undo me, Nina knew how to say in a way that made his hair stand up. With Claire never anything even close.

I need to live forever, Ned thought.

11 "I don't know why we're here," Ned said to Gruen as they stood in the living room, waiting for the sliding doors to the formal dining room to open and reveal the sumptuous breakfast they all expected. Preparations were still in progress. Premium coffee was plainly going to be on the menu.

"She's going to tell us why we're here," Gruen said. He was medicated. The day was warm and everyone had gotten into jeans and sport shirts. Joris's shirt was tucked in. He was showing off a little. He was the only one of them in short sleeves. He had been a little late in joining them to wait for breakfast, delayed by his push-up regimen and whatever else he did without fail.

At the end of the sofa was a woven African basket the

size of a washtub containing a midden of scholarly quarterlies, most still in their mailing sleeves. Ned thought, After NYU we were supposed to keep up with the quarterlies because they represented a worthy stream of thought nobody was paying much attention to. He had tried, in a sampling way, until the branch libraries in Contra Costa County had stopped letting periodicals circulate, meaning readers would have to sit in a chair at the library and fit the experience into the ever-shrinking hours the library was open. And then the subscription list had dwindled down to the *Sewanee Review*. Vandalism had been the announced reason for cutting back on periodicals, something he had difficulty imagining applied to the *Explicator* or *Celtic Studies*.

Gruen asked, "Got any water on you?" which was not exactly a normal question. Gruen had a pill bottle in his hand which he rattled in explanation. Just then the doors slid open.

It was indeed another feast. Places were set around an exaggerated refectory table. Iva was in black. She was at the head of the table. Elliot was directing two women servers, new people, older women. Elliot was wearing a black business suit. He was scheduled to meet with the authorities. Joris made some effort to secure the seat on Iva's right.

Iva was repaired. She seemed calm. All the food was hot. There were warming panels in use. Ned's scrambled eggs were hot. Even the tomato and scallion garnish was hot. Ned sat down next to Gruen, mid-table. There were four or five media people present, to whom he hadn't been introduced.

"Don't miss the mushroom thing," Gruen said.

Ned realized that Iva was looking with some intensity

at him. A strong and unwelcome feeling came over him. It was the conviction that he could help this woman, that the accidents of his life had peculiarly qualified him to help her in her sadness. It was unsettling.

Ned concentrated on eating. He thought that these might really be the best scrambled eggs he'd ever had. It couldn't be just the fines herbes because Nina used them routinely on eggs. Nina loved food but she didn't like to cook, which wasn't that unusual. Unexpectedly, Iva rapped on the table.

She said, "I don't know how I can thank you for coming so quickly here . . . as you can see I am lost. Here."

Ned wanted to kill Gruen, who was taking a large second portion of eggs for himself but doing it with an excruciating slowness intended to make what he was doing less obvious. Part of the maneuver was to keep his eyes fixed on Iva while his arm worked independently like an animal for which he had no responsibility.

Iva said, "I present myself to you.

"I must do something.

"My life is black . . ."

Elliot intervened. He said, "Iva will talk individually later to you, one at a time, later. In the sun room."

"What sun room?" Ned asked Gruen in a whisper.

"I'll show you," Gruen said.

But Iva wanted to say more. She said, "You, you were his true friends. I won't stop now, Elliot. And you were more his friend than I was, you men, I have to say. I have to say that, yes." She began wringing her hands. Elliot was walking distractedly around the table, driving his hands deep into his pants pockets. He appeared to be talking to himself.

Iva said, "We must make a . . . *book*." She was imploring them.

Elliot said, "Well she doesn't mean a book per se, she means a memorial collection . . . statements . . ."

"Yes, but in a *book*," Iva said.

Elliot said, "She means she wants it *bound*. That's what she means."

"Eulogies?" Joris asked.

Iva said, "Yes, but *more*. We must *say* them, and it must be the truth, you see."

Gruen said, "I think she means a ceremony."

Joris was saying something calming to her, and it seemed to be helping. Iva rose and the guests followed suit. The breakfast had been very truncated.

Now Elliot was saying that individual meetings with Iva would start in half an hour. Ned joined Iva and took her hand. He said, "Why don't you take me second or third so I can take care of something first."

"What is it?" she asked.

"Nothing, just something I need at the Vale. The *Times*."

Iva covered his hand with hers and squeezed with a certain ferocity. She said, "You can go. You can go if you have to. But just be sure you don't take the top paper on the pile he has, but take the next under. You see they let their filthy dog sleep on the papers."

Elliot said, "Man there is no problem. We're getting the *Times* delivered here starting today. *Washington Post*, too. And one last thing, you're all coming out of the tower and over here."

Introductions to the strangers, most of whom were from *Deutsche Welle*, were managed by Elliot. Ned knew that he wasn't going to remember the names. They all looked young to him.

12 Elliot was leading Ned to his meeting with Iva when something disconcerting happened. In a recess in the living room wall between the end of the interminable sofa and a door to somewhere else in the Winchester Mystery House that this was, hung a framed full-length portrait of Iva and Douglas in late youth, in oil. Elliot veered off toward it and seemed to be brushing its surface smartly with his open hand. But that wasn't what he was doing: he was flicking away a pushpin that someone had stuck into it. There was a lamp fixture on the top of the frame. Ned halted in front of the painting. He fiddled with the fixture but the bulb seemed to be dead.

Anyway, there he was, Douglas. There seemed to be lots of punctures in the surface. Who would have done that? Elliot was pulling at him. Recently Nina had said, Know what I hate? . . . puncture wounds.

Elliot said to come on. "Who did this?" Ned asked. Elliot was impatient and pulled at him.

Douglas's ludic period had extended well beyond NYU. The double portrait, done in a photorealist mode by some artist whose name he should doubtless know, was a goof. There he was, Douglas, in safari kit, shirt and shorts and boots and thick socks up to the knee, standing unnaturally straight, separate from and not touching his wife, a miniature umbrella of the kind they put in mai tais held between the thumb and forefinger of his languidly dangling left hand. In back of the couple it was sea and cumulus. Iva was wearing sunglasses. Light blond, he would say her hair was then, and it was swept up and fixed in a sort of fan. She was wearing a black caftan with fragments of mirror sewn into it. And there were images of interest showing in the fragments if you had the time to look. He identified Mick Jagger in one of them, and, surprisingly to Ned, he saw an image of Claire. Douglas was his thin, willowy, standardly handsome second-lead self. His hair was combed straight back, flat against his head, and glistened with something like pomade. The artist had caught the quality of latent surprise that was always resident in Douglas's main expression, had always been there. Nobody was smiling. Ned thought, Fahn fahn fahn on the autobahn. And the name for Iva's sunglasses was harlequin. Nina would be interested in the details.

He and Elliot moved on.

It was nice, this new room. The main vista was of a wooded gorge. Iva had her back to it. She was seated in a voluminous rattan armchair and pointing to its twin, which was set close to hers, at an angle and at a fairly intimate distance, in his opinion. She had a stack of papers in her lap. There were more papers in an accordion file between her bare feet. Iva's all-black outfit was, he thought, a little shiny for the circumstances. Maybe it was satin. She was wearing silver bracelets.

Elliot was in a corner using his cell phone. Ned had gotten a look at what Elliot was calling "the hub," a room loaded with telephones, fax machines, and computers. He waved to Ned and left them, still engaged in his phone work.

"Have you a cigarette?" she asked Ned, in a hushed voice.

"Hey I'm sorry. I don't smoke. Due to Douglas, by the way." It was something he was grateful for, genuinely.

"I don't either," she said, holding a hand up and making a wiping motion. "No it's just now. A little. You understand."

Everybody around them had smoked in the seventies, at college. *Against Sameness!* could have been their group's motto. And probably that sentiment as much as Douglas's idiosyncratic interest in alternative medical notions had been behind the pressure to get them all to quit. Plainly Elliot had relapsed. One of Douglas's more convincing faxes explained the handful of almonds Ned tried to remember to eat each day.

Ned said, "There's lung cancer on both sides of my family. It was a gift, when I quit. I was smoking Kools at the time and Douglas had a medical photograph of the lungs of a menthol cigarette smoker, and that worked for me."

"I like Marlboros," she said. He could barely hear her.

Mist had flowed into the gorge and stalled there. It was beautiful. He said, "How are you doing? That's an inevitable question and I know the answer. I'm sorry I even asked. You know how we all feel, Iva . . ."

She had lifted her chin up and tilted her head back. He felt the gesture showed her trying to keep the tears in. He didn't know what to say. He noticed that she had a fine, straight, short, horizontal dent in the upper round of her cheeks. He'd seen that in some famous face, Russian, pre-war cinema. He couldn't think of the star's name.

Ned said, "I went to the ravine." She flinched. He

shouldn't have said that. It was almost as stupid as Gruen having mentioned at breakfast his recollection that Douglas's favorite Poe story was "The Premature Burial."

One of the kitchen women came in, exchanged signs with Iva, and left.

"She will bring coffee," Iva said.

A big trope with Douglas had been knowing the names, and as much as seemed appropriate and practical about the servers and helpers and cleaners, the security guards, all the support workers who kept life so pleasant for the student body at NYU. He had been kind of ostentatious about it, but over time it had seemed like the right thing to do, and the working rabble, as Douglas had referred to them, seemed to appreciate it. Ned had carried this practice on in a dilute way in his life and Nina just did it by reflex. Of course Douglas had hated some of the rabble, like Pugnacio, as Douglas called Ignacio, their irascible super in the building on Second Avenue.

Iva was speaking to him and he needed to pay attention. She said, "May I tell you what I am hoping? Thank you. You were the closest to Douglas of all . . ." Ned hid his surprise.

She said, "Oh yes, you! He said so. You were the one he admired, with your work. Oh, your college group. You were interesting, all of you. But he would say it was Ned carrying on with the idea of the group." She touched his knee. "Don't look so strange. I'm telling you what he believed."

Ned felt murderous. The thinnest of threads had been thrown to him, and thinner and thinner, risible little things, risible invisible. And Douglas had never given a dime out of his fortune to Fair Trade or any of the other causes he brought to the group's attention. At one time or another, all the others had.

She said, "You were the closest, of course, because you both loved Claire." Something steely came into her voice.

Ned was shaken. He said, "I wasn't really in close contact with Douglas, you know. Especially after . . . well, things happened. You know." It was true he had loved Claire. And then he hadn't loved her. And it was also true that whenever he'd been close to saying to Claire that maybe they should think about splitting up, she had come up with a gift for him, a getaway trip, something personal that stopped the impetus. Sometimes a confession of a trivial sort would do the trick for her.

There was something possessed about what Iva was doing. She said, "Claire would write at times, you know. We would hear about your work. Your book, she sent it to us."

Now he was both enraged and astonished.

"My book?" He knew he was sounding rigid.

"Yes, about Mexico. The movement."

Ned had self-published his master's thesis on the ejido movement in Mexico, or rather on its death-throes. It wasn't even letterpress. It had typos. He doubted he had three copies left. It was paperback. All this had been years ago. She'd had no right to send his thesis to them.

He couldn't believe it. Something diabolical had gone on that he didn't deserve.

He said, "She wrote to you?" Immediately he regretted saying it. Because he had cut himself off from the position that he knew all about it and it was nothing, which would have left him a shred of dignity. But then probably he had done the right thing by admitting his ignorance, because the letters themselves would have declared that fact.

"She wrote to Douglas. We have her letters. He admired you both."

He thought, Great, he admired us because we lived at the material level of graduate students. In the name of something. Ned was drowning in bitterness. And now he was wondering about something else, Claire's little windfalls, little freshets of cash every now and then, things she got at thrift shops that looked too good for what she claimed she'd spent. Birthdays, cash from family members even though she was estranged from pretty much every single one of them. Don't be inventing things, he said to himself. He had to get away from this. He got up but sat down again immediately. They weren't through. The kitchen woman brought mugs of coffee on a tray. He was going to stop thinking of Iva's staff people as retainers. And he had to stop being a dumb prick about people living so fucking comfortably. He had lived his life a certain way, so enough.

Iva said, "What I want is that you tell the story of Douglas's *mind*. From your school days. His ideas . . .

"Others can tell about his work, about Kundera. The other things the public knows. Elliot can do that.

"We are going to make a magnificent event to remember him. You are the ones to speak, because . . . I can't, myself."

He was afraid that she was about to weep. She picked up her coffee and inhaled the aroma. He waited.

She said, "I have not been a good wife to Douglas. It's a bad story."

She gestured broadly, and said, "All this will be gone."

"What?" Ned said.

"A foundation might take this place, that is possible."

Her purpose, with him—if that's what it had been—seemed to have been accomplished. The news she had given him was like acid. The membranes between things in his mind that should be kept separate were being eaten away. He could think of a few more things he would like to know about Claire. He wouldn't ask. He would not.

He asked, "So did Claire stop by here on a trip, ever?"

Iva appeared to hesitate over her answer. He hated it. Finally she said, "Oh yes, but not very often. I would say, at the most, six times she was here. And she might call from New York. She traveled."

Rise above this, Ned said to himself. "Yes, she did travel. Well, I'm, I have to say, surprised. Douglas *dropped* her. She was not a forgiving person. Of course I only know her side of it. And it wasn't something she wanted to talk about. She made clear. Well. Jesus."

He saw some relaxation or satisfaction come into her expression. It wasn't pleasant.

This has to stop here, he thought. He had to leave.

"I'll do what's necessary," he said.

"You'll write it out first, for me," she said.

"All right," he said. It was time to go.

13 He had guessed high blood pressure for Gruen and he'd been correct. He put his arm around Gruen's shoulder. They were walking to the accident site together.

The world was wet. It was much warmer. Rags of fog drifted overhead.

They were almost at the scene. Joris was lagging a few yards back. Ahead there was nothing to see, just the hill dropping lower and then the place it broke. The sheared-off earth that had fallen into the creek bed was being washed downstream, cut in two places by the surging waters. The Toro riding mower had been winched up out of the viscous mass choking the creek and left to stand alone farther up the hill on the grass, like a monument. It had been draped in plastic and wrapped around haphazardly with yellow barrier tape. Ends of the tape flapped festively when the wind struck. The far bank of the creek looked normal. It was steep. Thick woodland began just behind the drop on that side. The ground abutting the catastrophe was very torn up: ordinary rubble and broken bricks and chunks of scrapwood showed in it, evidence, maybe, of the quality of the topsoil Douglas had trucked in to raise and contour the hilltop during his program of estate improvement. There were metal stakes here and there. Broad tire tracks scored what was left of the lawn near the site.

Without warning, Gruen dropped to his knees. Ned aborted a motion to reach out after him and pull him back from the edge. It wasn't necessary. Gruen got up, black spots on the knees of his jeans. Ned saw that he hadn't been that close to the edge, in fact.

"Say something," Gruen said. He was weeping. In the group, in the past, Gruen had been everybody's confessor. Ned knew he hadn't been paying proper attention to Gruen, not seriously, over the years. The most you could say is that he had been keeping track of him. "Say something," Gruen said again.

Ned didn't know what to say. A dry sob came out of him and he said, "Venice is sinking." He didn't know why.

They seemed to know what he meant, his friends.

14

Something called the Vale was just ahead of her.

Nina thought, Don't be insecure. She was having a new fear. It was neurotic and it was about Ned and Iva. It was shameful, but fortunately she had no shame. It was a pattern, a potential pattern, she was afraid of. She thought, There are people so physically extraordinary that if they're for any reason willing to stay with you and be your love you take their shit forever. Claire when she became good riddance still had her perfect skin, which was perfect due to her avoidance of facial expressions. The great Douglas limited himself to great beauties. And Iva was supposed to be beautiful in an ornate Austro-Hungarian way, at least judging by the images on the net from her Prague days and more recently from the jacket of her latest children's book *Hans and the Miles Long Knockwurst* or whatever the fuck she called it. So, as to Ned . . . Number One, her great beauty. Number Two, she was in some kind of distress, which is always attractive. And Number Three, she had a readymade offspring. She had already proven that she produced babies. On the other hand Iva was forty-three. On the *other* hand, she herself would hit forty before you could say God help me.

What in the name of fuck was the Vale? It looked like an establishment that had come through a time machine with stuff clinging to it from different eras. It was built in a lovely swamp. It was the place she could get a taxi to carry her up to the castle, she'd been told, so she loved it. She toiled forward. Her next roll-on carryon would have larger wheels. That would be superior when rolling your belongings through muck.

She was too tired. She had spent the night in Kingston in a motel from hell. She thought, I stayed in a room that was rejected by the people who made *The Cabinet of Dr. Caligari* because it was too scary: I'm going to tell Ned that.

She had to get to Ned. And she had to look good.

15 "This happened," Gruen said. "Where you were, I don't know. This was thirty minutes ago."

Ned said, "I was indisposed. Go ahead."

Gruen said, "Well, this happened. Outside the kitchen there's a deck and a hatch and stairs that lead down to another deck. On the lower one you're out of sight and private and you can enjoy the sound of the creeks the livelong day. So there Iva was on a bench and looking very shaky to me. I asked if she was all right and she stood up and asked if I was a smoker by any chance.

"Well I am, I hate to admit. I'm way cut down, but I am. I said something about this being a time when you can be forgiven if you take a drag or two. And I told her, which was the truth, that I didn't have any smokes on me.

"So *she* said Here, I'll give you one. I only have two. We'll share. We'll split and later you'll get a pack for me when you go to the store next. Oh, and Marlboro is what I prefer but it doesn't matter.

"And she took a lighter out of her pants pocket and then right in front of me she pushes her hand into her cleavage and comes out with two Marlboros and gives me one. It was warm and it smelled like her. I was pretty stunned but I pretended that this was the way I always got my cigs, of course. So we lit up, tra la! I was sorry for her. She smoked the thing like a machine."

Ned said, "Outré," which was not a word he'd used since 1974.

Gruen said, "Some people are kind of magnificent. Just an observation."

16 Ned was running. It was downhill and steep and the road was what it was and he was trying to be careful. *Nina* was at the Vale, waiting for him. The message had come to the house. Elliot had gotten it. The message was that she could get a taxi but only as far as some bridge, so she was waiting for someone from the estate to come down in a car and pick her up at the store, unless that was unreasonable. When Elliot read him the message Ned turned south and began to run. He could get down to the Vale faster than he could organize the loan of a car. Also he wanted to run. Nina was insane to do this, but she was here.

It was safer to run on the crown of the road than in the ruts or on the margin. How was she going to like all this forest primeval, so dank, so endless. She was insane.

She was going to be a wreck, exhausted, how would she look?

Now everything was going to be impossible, but better.

Ned turned onto the spur path that led to the Vale's parking area and he could see Nina there. He halted to get his breath. She had seen him and was waving as she mounted a low, broad tree stump at the edge of the lot. She began posing. The stump was a plinth for herself as a living statue representing Wrath. She put a fist on her hip and raised her other fist high in the air. The upraised fist became a claw. She was crazy. But it was going to be all right. She was letting him know he was forgiven, definitely. Yes, she was, she was letting him know. The old burgomaster was on the porch in his wheelchair. She didn't care who saw what she was doing. There was something to be said for a little idiosyncrasy in the world. Her carryon was leaning against the stump, mud-caked.

She looked fine. Her black hair was done up in a tall bun whose crest was visible over the crown of her head. It was unusual for her, and probably intended to make her look taller, like the heels on the cowboy boots she was wearing.

He was close now. He could see that her eyes were done. She knew how to do makeup when she wanted to, by god. She was wearing tight new jeans and her fringed buckskin jacket, which carried a definite cowgirl reference, which was all right. The rather fierce first impression her small sharp face could give was softened by fatigue.

He jumped up onto the stump with her and embraced her so hard they tottered for a moment.

"I came here to kill you," she said.

"I know. I know. I'm sorry."

"How sorry are you?"

"So sorry, but we're forgiving each other, right?"

"Not yet. I'm not going to kill you, I'm going to fuck you."

"Absolutely."

"That is your punishment."

"I know. And I'm so sorry the way I left. My heart is shaking."

He was squeezing her. He was full of joy. They had to get down from there. She was pressing his crotch with the back of her hand. She did anything she wanted to. He wasn't hard. Afloat, he felt *afloat*.

"Hm," she said.

"Don't worry, my dear."

He pulled her hand up and against his chest. He said, "Feel my heart."

"Feel mine," she said, and pressed his hand against the front of her bright yellow linen shirt, his favorite.

They had to stop this.

He renewed his embrace in order to keep his balance.

"Unhand my behind," she said.

17 They had decided to proceed by stages up to the property, pulling her luggage and stopping to rest as much as they needed to, taking their time and talking, catching up. She'd said she loved all the trees, but described them as excessive, to make him laugh. She wasn't above using a witticism twice if she thought he'd missed it the first time or had insufficiently appreciated it. She had no shame about it, in fact she thought doing that was funny.

They were at the bridge. She said, "I want to tell you something so I can forget it. You can help me. I had to squeeze past a woman in the aisle on the plane and I thought she was making a face at me so I made a face back at her, just before I realized she was exophthalmic. I feel

awful. I want you to make it fade from my mind. I want it
to fade so completely there's not a trace. So make it fade."

"I'm doing it."

Nina said, "Tell me when it's completely gone."

They laughed.

They were kissing again. "It's good you didn't wear lip-
stick," he said.

"Thinking ahead," she said. She was neatening him up.
She'd once said that makeup was advertising for your vagina
and hers was taken. He'd liked that remark even if it wasn't
serious, because she was his.

One thing he'd learned from her, that she'd learned
from the burgomaster, was that there was another road, a
much longer back way up the hill that avoided the torrents
and was used by trucks and emergency service vehicles.
And she had brought him up to date on the Convergence.
There was a solid consensus that the talking points would
use Invasion but not Anglo-Saxon Invasion. He'd taken the
position that that was what it was going to be, literally, even
if the Spaniards were brought in to put a mustache on it. It
was going to be Americans, Brits, and a few Australians but
no French.

They crossed the bridge. Nina wanted to know what
Douglas had meant when he said he lived in a dying forest.

Ned said, "He was being melodramatic. There was an
ash blight. The other trees were fine. And maples were the
successor species, so it ended up greener than before."

Ned moved his attention to the urgent question of
accommodations, meaning a decent bed, not a cot, and privacy. It had to be solved.

18 It had taken only a second's observation to dismiss the tower accommodations as impossible. She was a pest when it came to beds. She knew it. She was a mattress hog and was used to articulating her body for sleep employing an army of pillows which was why their mattress at home took up three-quarters of the bedroom. If she had to, she would lie down on an ironing board to conceive, but she strongly preferred not to.

Ned was a genius at logistics when he wanted to be. She needed him to be a genius now. He needed to start machinating immediately. She looked at his crotch. She had gone overboard with the teasing, obviously, given that he now had to go forth and interact.

"Recede," she said, addressing his lower self.

19 He was a genius and this was a coup.

He was slightly hyperventilating as he locked the cabin door behind them, triumphant. He had proved his ingenuity his desire his what-have-you, in spades . . . and his, well, erectitude because here he was, getting hard again. Nina wanted more kissing. It had taken a certain power, what he had done.

What he had done was, he had executed a continuous single flourish ending where they were, safe and private together. He had gotten Nina up the hill, had her wait out of sight in the tower, sought out the head housekeeper, a new persona, Mrs. Murphy, and laid out to her that his wife was here and that they urgently needed their own place, and getting a key from her for the unused pristine cabin expressly built for the boy, Hume. He had been delicate but frank with Mrs. Murphy, a thin, older, darker, sighing woman he guessed to be a Filipina. Elliot had approved the arrangement, frantic as he had been with phones ringing in the hive of industry that was the cockpit of everything going on. Since anything that might delay conjugation felt unbearable, he'd avoided Joris and Gruen.

This Wendy house was one of the many custom living setups Douglas had tried to sell to his impossible son over the years. There had been boarding schools of various kinds including a brief spell in something in Saugerties called a Hof, which had been a facility run for the youth wing of an Odinist pagan organization. Then there was the boy's yurt. And a room somewhere in the manse, too. So they had created this House of His Own, and he'd rejected it.

"That's right, manhandle me," Ned said as Nina clung to him while he edged them into the bedroom. There were two rooms, a small main room and a bedroom, and what would have to be called a kitchenette, and a bathroom. The smell of fresh paint hung in the air. Some of the window panes still bore manufacturers' stickers. The walls were pale gray, window frames white, the floors gleaming amber pine. The main room housed an old steel desk, a chair, and a bookcase with one paperback in it, *Weird Shadows Over Innsmouth*, by H. P. Lovecraft. The kitchen had seemed to be equipped with the basics, although there was no food in the countertop refrigerator. There was a stack of new window screens awaiting installation. In the bathroom it had been similar: towels, facecloths, soap still in its wrapper, an electric fan and an electric heater, both still boxed. The windows were uncurtained. The ceiling lights functioned and there was a gooseneck lamp on a stool near the head of the bed. So they could read when their revels were over that night. Good. The bed linen was fresh. In fact, it was new.

You could begin a new life in a place like this, which had probably been the idea, Ned thought. He imagined himself arriving with a toothbrush and a pad and pencil and sitting down to stare out at the verdure, nothing on his agenda, which reminded him that he had to find a way to cover the bedroom windows with towels, somehow. Nina was continuing with undressing him. To put up the towels he needed pushpins or a hammer and nails, and right away. Nina was being herself. She ceased long enough for him to collect a few towels and she joined him in clamping the top edge of the towels between the sashes and the casing on each of the windows looking into their bedroom. It wasn't a neat job, but it would do.

Nina resumed her attentions, undressing him without his assistance, slowly, like the devil incarnate she was.

Nina wanted him naked but she liked herself to be half-dressed for the proceedings. She dropped her buckskin jacket to the floor. She liked to be taken in dishevelment, with her underwear askew or undone, outer garments barely obscuring her naughty bits.

She finished undressing him, kissing his genitals when she felt like it.

20 When had *buck* naked turned into *butt* naked? Nina wondered. And when had it become common for women to refer to their own breasts as *boobs*, and as casually as they might refer to their elbows or ears?

She had resisted sleep. It was midafternoon. Ned was dozing. Their limbs were still entangled. Something she liked was waking up with Ned and finding that they were in new combinations and alignments, compositions devised by their unconscious minds while they slept. Once she'd awakened to find that the soles of her feet were pressed firmly against his. She wanted everything to go on forever if possible.

Meticulously and with strategic halts she disengaged from Ned. He could sleep some more. She was feeling almost perfect. Ned had come twice. She had a good feeling about the first shot especially. She was using the word *womb* a lot in her ruminations lately. Ned had been all heat and conviction. And she should be doing one of her dumb visualizations, shouldn't she, à la her womb becoming a flowerpot suddenly exploding with geraniums? She didn't feel like it. As a young girl she'd visualized her heart as a dark red artichoke and the leaves as things her future boyfriends would strip away and it would be dramatic.

She was supposed to have her legs above her head by this time. Okay she was pinching her introitus shut. Now to get on with it.

She studied her sleeping man. There was something she understood, which was why Ned had felt so urgently the need to fly east. It had to do with power. It had to do with the old days, with the dismal Roman Catholic miasma of his household, the Catholic spell over his mother and his brother, the deathly house he was raised in, the early death of his father, his escape to NYU and meeting Douglas and being included in the power group of friends. That had been his great escape, as he saw it. Right now it was like a fable where some grail or amulet has been mislaid and needed to be gotten back by a hero going into a labyrinth or dark gorge the hero had already passed through once. Oops he forgot his amulet in the gorge and has to go back. She had a better idea of what he was doing than he did. He wasn't depressed but he wasn't happy enough. The fucking truth was that Ned was in *fact* an instrument for good, both in Fair Trade and before, in the co-operative movement . . . what was left of it. But he could be more of a force! He was a skeptic on the subject of himself. It held him back. It was painful to her. She shook the thought away.

She had inched herself to a sitting position on her edge of the bed. Her next feat was going to be achieving a three-quarter shoulder stand without waking her husband up. She swiveled around and raising her pelvis she levered her feet up the wall at the head of the bed. When she felt the angle was steep enough she let go of her vulva. She held the position. She was dogged. Should she throw in some visualization? It was too boring. She would distract herself otherwise. "You guys are adorable," she murmured to her breasts. Ned was a fiend for her breasts. It was almost a dream state he went into. She was reminded that there was an amount of hair on Ned's back she might suggest doing something about, if he were somebody else.

Getting fucked was so interesting, seen from the peculiar detached mental moment that could descend on her during the act. She felt a flash of fellowship with all women getting fucked, the ones getting fucked carelessly or badly or cruelly, the ones fucked decently or brilliantly. She thought of the shadow of night sliding around the globe endlessly, and with the fall of night the clashing of a million cymbals sounding and representing the coming together of males and females in the Continue Humanity project, this colossal enterprise. But that was enough. There was too much blood in her head.

She let herself relax off the wall. She lay with her knees up for a while, and then turned on her side, sensing suddenly that something was wrong. One of the towels was moving. Where it had been clenched between the sash and casing, something was dragging it minutely to one side leaving naked glass along the edge of the window and then there was an eye and part of a face in that space and then that was gone. It was gone before she could gasp. She was freezing. Violently she caught the sheets up against her and in the process woke Ned.

21 He hadn't run this fast since his last field day at Frick Junior High. He was running in an attempt to lay hands on the only child of an old friend who was dead. Life was unusual.

Peeping at naked people without their permission was a crime. He could understand an adolescent doing it, but still. When he'd realized what it was Nina was trying to tell him he'd jammed himself into his clothes. His loafers were meant to be worn with socks, not bare feet.

He stopped to finish buttoning his shirt and to get his breath. He could see Hume. This was a lower part of the hill where the lawn had given way to brush, down past the place Douglas's life on earth had ended. His quarry, which is what Hume was, appeared intermittently. He was on the opposite side of the stream that was roaring its way toward the flatlands. Hume was scrambling nimbly up and away through the vegetation. Douglas would have been proud.

He was tired. He'd scared Hume, which was all he could do for now. He didn't know if there was something generically wrong with the next generation or not. You can't lift a cheesecake with an iron hook, somebody had said. Hume was tearing his way out of sight. He was gone. Ned turned back. Nina was coming to join him.

Sex with Nina was so . . . great. And there was no work to it. Claire had thought of her own body as a votive object.

"I wish you wouldn't run," she said when she reached him.

"Why not?"

"You could fall. People fall and die around here." She swept her hand in the direction of the raging brook. There were slick boulders spaced across the brook that only an idiot would use to cross over. She pointed at them. "Look, you might have tried to jump on those youyouyou, my man of action, my man of action guy. Good thing I came . . . What's *wrong* with that boy?" She was wearing a man's engulfing white terrycloth robe and flip-flops.

"I don't know. What Joris said is that they were going to try homeschooling again. Hume told his mother he's a follower of Odin. They're a pagan group and their religion is based on Norse mythology. The whole deal is right wing."

Nina was a proud person. He had to remember about

not over-explaining things to her. She was self-conscious
about her two-year community college education but she
knew more than anybody, really, and certainly more than
Claire, and Claire had a PhD. It would be good not to
spend too much time thinking about fucked-up children.
Only children, like Hume, seemed to be the biggest risk
and their child was likely to be a one and only.

She said, "You must be cold."

Here it came. She had a fixation about being dressed
warmly at all times, not only herself but the world. There was
nothing annoying about it, or there shouldn't be, because it
came from nothing worse than out-of-control empathy. It
was part of her character. She was also crazed about bedclothes, blankets. She tended to want more coverage than
he did and she would frequently insist or at least imply that
she knew better how comfortable he was going to be with
his choice of blanket layers than he did. She laughed when
he accused her of making too many blanket statements.

They came to a decision. They would go back to the
cabin, where he would scotch-tape paper towels onto the
windowpanes, two layers if he went outside and could see
anything. They would make tea.

She led the way back. She was doing something. She
was torquing around in the cavernous robe she had on. She
was making good time.

Her underpants dropped to the ground and she kicked
them to the side, striding straight ahead. He picked them
up, noted the teardrop-shaped wetness in the crotchpiece,
balled them up, and put them in a pocket.

They strove upward in silence. A couple of moments
later, it was her bra. It was black, a new one. He retrieved it.

"I'm smiling," he said.

. . .

She was in the bathroom.

After a moment, she said, "Shit."

"What is it?"

"I'm marveling at the feebleness of this shower and how much I don't care anyway."

He went to see. The water spraying out of the showerheads smelled old or stale. It wasn't foul. Later he could unscrew the fixture and make the flow normal. He assumed the odor would go away, with use.

He considered her there, in the shower stall.

"My breasts are looking at you," she said.

She was trying to keep him cheered up. After a baby the areolas of her perfect small breasts would take up more of the divine surface. At least that was what he expected to happen. Because she would nurse. That was already decided on. She'd once asked why men thought undressed women were not considered really naked if their nipples were obscured. He didn't know.

"How do you feel?" she asked.

"Well. Quoting somebody, A pleasant despair in the region of the loins."

"Why *despair*?"

"It's just a quote. Post coitum triste, maybe, but I don't really feel that. In fact I think maybe we struck pay dirt." He thought, You've struck *gold . . . fool's gold*: that's from something. He said, "But it's the female who gets the intuition, isn't it?"

"I'm not telling," she said.

She positioned herself so that the spray was playing directly on her face. Her hair was so long that he could grab it tight at the nape of her neck, twist up the fall, and mock-lash her with it, now and then.

"Look how much I'm not complaining," she said.

"Look how much you're repeating yourself. And get the fuck dressed. You have to meet people."

"I'll look nice. I'm putting on makeup."

"You don't have to."

"No I mean the right amount, about as much as for work."

"*That* much?" He said it gently.

He was sorry for women. Nina had a rather gnarled little toe she didn't like him to look at and she was standing awkwardly with her good foot on top of the toes of what she called her awful foot.

She pointed at his crotch. "Do you think you'll have time to give me my just deserts again, one more time?"

"That remains to be seen," he said, leaving the bathroom.

"Wait, my breasts are still filthy," she called. But he ignored her.

Nina was malingering. Some day someone would explain to her why everything had to be so difficult. She was supposed to be actively calm. And what if he returned with that juvenile delinquent to deal with.

Ned was competent. The windows were satisfactorily covered. And he was interesting. He'd asked her if she thought it meant anything that his favorite toy as a child had been a little tin periscope. She'd said she didn't think so. And then he'd gone on about how long he'd been willing to secrete himself behind a sofa and wait for something to happen in the living room. And she'd said Well it shows once again your long attention span, but frankly, re a child, it was about as interesting as saying he was fascinated by secret passages and buried treasure. He wanted to tell her things. And then there was this: there had been a girl in the third grade named Lynn who wore a locket he was curious about. She was flirtatious, as in making an undue number of references to her behind, but with everybody. And she flaunted, if that's the word, her locket, during these suggestive behaviors. And nobody knew what was in the locket. And then this and that had happened and he had gotten closer to her than the other boys had, and she'd said she was going to show him something secret—the contents of her locket. And what had been in the locket was, she'd explained, a collection of her desiccated scabs, from wounds that had healed, and he'd said that there had been something intimate about it and that in fact he'd felt like running around the play yard in some kind of triumph. Ned was increasingly into telling her the truth about everything. It was no wonder, because he'd been living for years with a piece of statuary. His mind was jammed with unshared reflections, memories . . .

The cabin was weird but maybe it was just right. He'd done a neat job with the paper towels and typing paper, on the windows. When she looked around she thought of shoji screens and kabuki.

22 She was always doing something, Nina. Somewhere in the cabin she had found a tiny rabbit-eared black-and-white TV set. Earlier, she had tried to get a news program on it, without success. Now she was sitting

naked, crosslegged, on the bed, holding the thing out at arm's length, squinting at it.

She said, "It only works on this one channel and only in certain places in here, certain elevations, so to speak."

The reception was on the dappled side, but he was able to make out that she was watching an ice skating exhibition. A girl was doing a prolonged spin, head flung back.

Nina said, "I can do that for twenty minutes."

"You don't do it that often, I notice."

"Do you want to know why I don't?"

"Naturally."

"Because it makes me dizzy."

"Right."

He reminded her that she needed to get ready. He went outside again.

Hume was somewhere. So be it, Ned thought.

A little way down from the cottage a mossy granite hump about the size of a compact car stuck up out of the lawn. Ned was leaning against it. He had completed the last of the top nine calls required by Convergence business. *The marches were going to be immense.*

Moss had a distinct odor. I did not know that, he thought. The odor was like the smell of urine. He pushed himself away from the rock and bent to examine the lower surfaces of the monolith more closely. Someone may have peed on it, he thought, or an animal like a stag marking its territory.

He was keeping an eye on the cottage. Nina must be almost dressed. She knew where he was waiting and that the paper-covered windows would let her put on a shadow play for him. She was doing it. They could doubtless get some actual curtains from the manse, if it mattered.

He stretched. It was still misty. He wanted Joris to sign the petition, and the others, too, but especially Joris. He shouldn't be assuming he knew where his friends stood politically, based on the past. If only his personal dark sense of what it was going to be like this time could be instilled in other minds by some kind of contagion, that would help. But he didn't have that gift. Douglas had once had it. He himself could help once the ball got rolling. He could help with the arrangements and he was always willing to be on the cleanup committee. He felt his pilot light was back on. The standard munitions the U.S. Army used were made from recycled radioactive metal. He hadn't mentioned *that* to Joris, the new the hideous *permanent* consequences of just blowing things up. The only bad news he'd gotten during his calls was that some absolute idiot had approached ISKCON about joining the East Bay march and ISKCON had seemed interested. He was not going to have the Hare Krishnas involved if he could help it.

He walked up to the bedroom window, tapped on it, and then stepped back. Nina posed, making a cruciform shadow, which meant, he guessed, that she was ready for her debut.

He wanted to delay everything. He wanted to get up on a big rock and hold his arms out like Nina, like the Gandhi of the Catskills or the Jesus overlooking Rio de Janeiro.

Three of the nine people he'd talked to on the phone had asked him if he was all right. He'd explained about Douglas's death to everyone, but still what they wanted was some more evident elation out of him when he got the repeated majestic estimates for participation in the Convergence. He was elated, but apparently not enough. Rise, he said to himself. *A day of streets like rivers of fists* was from a poem.

After Nina's ablutions, Ned had gotten the shower to work better by unscrewing the head and clearing it of a clot of matted leaf shreds. He should have done it before she'd used the thing. It had been a simple task. Nina was always nice about showing gratitude for small tasks, and it wasn't flattery. Ned knew he was benefitting by comparison with her all-talk ex-boyfriend Bob.

They were both cleaned up and ready, or thereabouts. In fact she was still busy on her hands and knees behind the bed.

"You know what I hate?" she said.

"I already do."

"Okay what?"

"Puncture wounds."

"*No*. What I hate is when you lose your shoes and have to look all over the place and when you find them it's just your shoes."

The deodorant she had brought smelled like pine. She apologized for its not being their customary scentless type. Ned said, "That's okay. In fact I like to use this kind once in a while. It makes me feel regular."

"Like the masses?"

"Right."

"Where are the masses when you need them?" she said.

"You'll see. Just wait."

They were both wearing jeans and black sweaters, which made no difference at all to her. Claire would have complained that they looked like twins. Hume was on his mind, still. Douglas's original plan had been to name his son Godwin, after William Godwin the cosmocreator of anarchism, ignoring the static the abbreviation of Godwin would have brought down on the child. Now Gruen was saying that in fact Douglas had been claiming in the last couple of years that his son hadn't been named for David Hume, as they all knew he had, but in honor of Hume Cronyn, the actor. What was the point of that? It was annoying.

It was time to go. There was something he wanted to tell Nina first, an item he was carrying around from his adolescence. Sometimes certain memories just emerged from his consciousness and if she was around, he could vent and be done. She had gotten used to it.

There was a secret he was going to keep from her, though. Before he had gotten into the shower they had tried again and to get hard he had resorted to an image of Iva, naked except for her apron, bending over and presenting a rear view to him.

Nina was finalizing the placement of barrettes in her hair. It was pulled straight back. She was looking at herself in the mirror. She said, "I need beauty treatments of some sort."

He approved everything about her appearance. He said, "Something I want to tell you. It doesn't exactly relate to Hume." Bringing this up from nowhere might soften the light on Hume, it occurred to him.

She sat down on the bed.

"Okay, I would shoplift paperback books from display racks in drugstores, mostly. Mostly science fiction. The racks were usually near the door and you could slip out quickly. Once I was getting set to take *Slan*, I think, but I got flustered and stole the wrong book, which turned out to be a thick little compendium of the plots and librettos of the great operas, something I had zero interest in. So but when I got home I was seized with the feeling I had to read the damned thing to justify taking it. I took science fiction for the pleasure of reading, so since I had this opera book in my possession some Catholic notion said I had to read it."

Nina said, "Aaah, so that's where you get all the minutiae about operas that you use when the subject comes up. You impressed me, you know!"

"Well then my crime was providential. Composer biographies were in there, too. A lot stuck. Is there anything you want to know about Donizetti?"

"Not right now. Are you saying this in defense of Hume, by the way?"

"I don't know." She would want to know more about his criminal past later. She identified him with a sort of unfailing law-abidingness.

"Was that the last one? Did you stop then?"

"No, I stole one more. From Holmes Bookstore in downtown Oakland. A big hardcover book, a history of stage magic by Ottokar Fischer, with big gorgeous plates. It was the maximum size I could fit down my pants. I wanted it and I put it down the front of my pants and pulled my stomach in and zipped my jacket over it and walked out of the place almost fainting. And that *was* the last, forever. I stopped before I was ever caught."

He could see that she was relieved.

She said, "His first name was Autocar?"

He said, "No, Ottokar, with an O and a K. Funny. Say

that's your name and you end up working as a mechanic in a garage? You know what that's called?"

"No."

"Nominative determinism. We collected examples. There was an insurance agent on Mercer Street named Justin Case. Douglas found them everywhere. The last name of a famous embezzler was Overcash. And there was a sewer commissioner whose last name was Dranoff."

"My life was uneventful. Shouldn't we go?"

23 There was the big house, all lit up in the gloaming. Nina seemed almost lighthearted. He imagined, just before they went in, Nina jumping up on his back and putting her legs around his waist, going in that way. She was so light and compact.

He didn't want to track water into the house. They both conscientiously ground their boot soles into the doormat.

24 She hoped she was ready. There were some particular facts in Ned's thumbnail portraits of his friends she should keep in mind. A cousin of David Gruen had died in the 9/11 horror. What else? Gruen was a Zionist. Elliot had been raised Bahai. She didn't know what was sacred to them, though. Supposedly Joris believed in nothing, so possibly she shouldn't insult the memory of Nietzsche or Robert Ingersoll, haha. Recently at lunch in a two-star hotel a colleague of hers had come back from the men's room to rejoin the group, saying It smells like

the Ganges in there. There had been two Hindu gentlemen among the diners who had ceased contributing to the conversation.

She wanted the friends to like her. She wasn't going to rub some holy foible the wrong way if she could help it. Be mindful, her mother would say. Once, after she and Bob had had a meal at Ma's, her mother had said Drive mindfully. Bob had been in the midst of a mildly New Age phase in his life and thought she was making fun of him. She had stayed with Bob mainly because leaving him would have revealed how she felt—about his being boring, oh God. The most exciting thing that had ever happened to Bob, judging from how often he mentioned it, had been finding a rubber band in his soup at Denny's. And then by the grace of God, he had cheated on her, so hosanna. She thought she was ready for the friends.

No one answered the door so Ned let them in. Here we are, she thought. Inside, Ned seemed to know where he was going. She wanted to have a relaxed look at the glamorous living room and its furnishings, but Ned took her quickly through a door and into a small room that felt like the world's greatest conversation pit. Around the walls ran continuous black leather sofa seating interrupted in only three places where there were doorways. Ned's hand was steady on her shoulder. This would be a good place for committee meetings. The back angle of the sofa would keep the committee members sitting up straight. And there was nice ivory ambient light, nothing like the bleaching fluorescence in library basements and union halls. The wood paneling suggested good acoustics.

She got it. The catlike way Ned was leading her along and why he had let them in after only a derisory bit of knocking on the door was so that he could surprise his friends with her, which was flattering.

He inched a door open and in effect popped her into the dining room ahead of him, saying, "Here she is."

And here they all were, standing around. One of them, Gruen, the heavy one, immediately began applauding in a friendly way. They had been contemplating the groaning board and waiting to eat. This was another perfect room. Ned's three friends came toward her, but moving much more quickly was Iva, who had entered from the kitchen bearing a loaded platter. She slid the platter onto the dining room table and then deftly got ahead of the men, holding her arms out to embrace her fellow woman. *Klimt!* Nina thought.

The brocade tunic, black and gold, and the black satin headband, Tartar eyes, multiplicity of finger rings, were Klimt, while *not-Klimt* were her sturdiness and her impressive and unfair bosom. I hate you, she thought.

Nina was saying how sorry she was about Douglas as the others were saying how glad they were to meet her and what an enormous and pleasant surprise it was to see her there. Iva stepped back. As she released Nina, she said, "*I want your hair.*"

Nina felt a moment of involuntary alarm. For a stupid instant, Nina had believed her hair was being requested as a hostess gift.

"Oh thank you," Nina said.

Iva's strong perfume was Klimt, to Nina. No, it was just European. The embraces all around ended. Iva's workout-calves looked very good. She was wearing snug Capri pants cuffed just below the knee.

Nina thought, Unfortunately some people are more like art objects than others and this woman is in that category and the category of people you find yourself not wanting to look away from because you might miss them in some fleeting and splendid moment. This woman was not a toy. Her face showed the marks of suffering, and something else, some iron drive. She was fully mobilized, was what Nina would say. Iva was grieving. She was grieving. And it was unfair to keep reading her. Nina looked for the faintest sign of age-parching in her grainless complexion. She saw nothing, and then she stopped. Iva was tall, but shorter than Ned, she could tell, who had thank God stopped answering, like a child, Five ten and a half, when he was asked his height.

Iva maneuvered people into the seating pattern she wanted. It was an enormous table. Iva was alone at the head, fanning herself with one hand and undoing the top of her tunic with the other. To her left was Joris and to her right, Elliot. Iva beckoned Nina to a place next to Elliot. Gruen was opposite Nina. Iva had put Ned next to Gruen. Ned got up, brought his chair around the end of the table, put it next to Nina, and went back for his place setting. There seemed to be acres of unemployed table space.

There was an actual wait-staff. Two older women were serving. The younger senior brought in two jumbo Erlenmeyer flasks into which wine had been decanted, red in one, white in the other. She began filling glasses around the table. The wineglasses were the capacious kind—Bordeaux glasses. Nina said no to wine. Gruen encouraged his server and ended up with two full glasses of red. Ned had a glass of white of which he would drink half. The enduring mystery of Hume . . . endured. She was not going to be the one to ask about that, but it was weird.

She felt the need to concentrate whenever Iva was speaking. Nina hadn't figured out what Iva was up to, yet— she was up to something. Her voice was on the low side, with a darling texture in the bottom ranges. A smoker's voice? It was easy to imagine Iva seductively wielding a cigarette during her adventures in intimate combat.

Nina was well aware that it was up to her to say something. She was blanking. Go, she thought. She tumbled into a formulation that began oddly with a statement about how sad she was to be there. She kept on. At one point she was asked to raise her voice. And she got through it, conscious the whole time of how much of the truth of her feelings she was leaving out. Everybody was looking at her, as she finished, with normal expressions. What she had wanted to convey was that she felt apologetic about inviting herself to the wake but that she'd felt that she had to do it in order to be with Ned when he was dealing with the loss of his great friend. That wasn't the true reason she was here, and this wasn't a wake, either. She didn't know exactly what the fuck kind of event it was supposed to be. Somebody was going to tell them soon.

Iva, in the midst of saying something reassuring to Nina, snapped her head around and hissed over her shoulder— startlingly to Nina—as a signal to the servers to bring in the salads. Nina wondered if the hissing was another European thing, because otherwise it was rude as shit. The salads came, bowls of bouffant butter lettuce and other good things.

Nina was asked about her trip. She avoided temptation

and understated unpleasantnesses along the way, like the deficits in amenity at the motel in Kingston where she'd spent the night. When she was through, she felt she'd gone on too long about the roadside distractions like the kaleidoscope as tall as a silo, the golem on display outside the ceramics studio, and the vast size of the two paintball dromes, the crumbling book barn where fallen siding let shelves of abandoned books show.

Everything was delicious. The conversation was normalizing, but Nina sensed that Iva was gathering herself for an act of some kind.

And it came. Iva stood up and rather violently unbuttoned her tunic and roughly shook herself out of it, complaining that it was too hot, she was having stress, it was too hot. Under the tunic she wore a low-cut black tank top, a little sprung along the neckline. Clearly they were all expected to join the complaint about the heat, but in fact no one else seemed to be too warm. Nina didn't feel too warm, in fact, the room felt a little chilly to her. Was Iva menopausal? She was forty-three, kind of young for it, but it was possible.

"I apologize," Iva said.

Joris was a good person. He took his jacket off in sympathy. He had a strong build, Nina thought. Then Ned annoyed her by taking his sweater off. God damn you, she thought.

Elliot tapped on a glass. He got up.

Under her breath, Nina said to Ned, "He's ashamed of something."

"Ashamed of *what*?"

"How do I know?" Nina said, regretting her observation.

"You brought it up."

"Can you keep your voice down?"

Elliot had a strong, carrying voice. "Listen, I'm sorry, but I have to ask everyone to move again. We have press, we have other media, we have some . . . individuals, as you'll see. A lot of people coming. Only a few are here yet. Today is Thursday, Friday and Saturday we prepare, Sunday the memorial. There'll be video people at work. Anyway.

"Tomorrow we need to sit down and plan. Saturday we go over what you've written and you rehearse."

Nina thought, The *otherness* of men but why go into it. He needs to say something personal about Douglas, but *first*, it has to be logistics.

Restiveness was developing among the friends. There was tension all over the place.

Elliot wasn't through. "Now about housekeeping . . .

"We need all of you in the manse. We need to use the whole tower, too. Nina and Ned, you come out of the cabin and there's a bedroom for you next to the bedroom Gruen and Joris are going to share. Sorry about the cabin but we need that, too. We have people to help you move after dinner. Anyway the beds over here are an improvement."

"Where are you sleeping?" Gruen asked.

Elliot was impatient. "You want to know where I'm sleeping? I'm sleeping on a futon in the media room with the phones, if you could call it sleeping."

Joris knocked on the table for attention. Nina wondered why this man had to go to prostitutes. He didn't seem the type, but possibly there *was* no type.

Joris said, "I'm telling you now I'm not writing something. I'll talk. I'll get up and talk, of course. You can put it on TV if you want to, fine. I'm talking not writing."

Elliot held his hands in the air. "Well we can sort this out. I don't know. Maybe you can read something."

"No," Joris said, half standing.

Iva put her hand on Joris's arm and leaned toward him. She had something for his ears only, apparently, and in the act of getting closer she hunched her shoulders forward minutely. Nina caught it.

"Oh my," Nina said to Ned, softly. But it was over before Ned could be a witness.

Something was mollifying Joris. He had kept his eyes in a proper direction during Iva's encroachment. Nina had seen him blush.

Nina realized she didn't know what she'd been eating. Everything had been delicious but her mind had been elsewhere. If she had to compliment Iva she wouldn't know what to compliment.

She told herself to grow up. She thought, We had butter lettuce salad cups with something in them and clam appetizers and green bean casserole and lobster risotto.

Elliot was a puzzle, with his long, waxy face. He was the tallest and the thinnest, but he had dog eyes.

She realized she had gone robot with her food because her mind had been on her inner sanctum. She could swear that she was having a faint prickling sensation there, which was impossible. But there was something physical. No more wine, no X rays. Maybe she was imagining it. If it persisted, she would call Ma.

The help were clearing.

Oddly, Gruen had left lumps of lobster on his plate. He'd eaten only the rice. And his clam appetizer was untouched and she wanted it. Was he being observant when it came to shellfish? Maybe he just wasn't hungry. She was worried for Ned that Gruen might not want to sign the petition. Hussein was the Bank of America for the families of Palestinian suicide bombers. Maybe nobody would sign, none of them. That was all Ned needed. It shouldn't hurt him but it would. She looked at Elliot again. Could she see any indications that he might not sign? How could she? She was being ridiculous. Well, he was wealthy and he was in the business and finance upper tier so it was possible that he wouldn't want to stand out, say, if the names of the signers got printed up in a *Times* ad. She didn't know if that was the plan. Elliot was being remote. But from everybody, not just Ned.

She could feel that Ned was preparing to say something to the group.

Ned said, "I think we should just speak out. Free-associate. Get a timer and we each say what we have to say."

Nina wanted to know what that might be. I am shuddering, she thought. Don't let it be some ghastly remake of their idiotic exhibitionism.

Gruen said, "Yes, we could read things. Anything. From emails he sent to that thing he wrote about comedy. You said you wanted something about that, Elliot."

"What thing about comedy?" Ned asked.

Joris said, "It wasn't something he wrote, it was an interview in *Der Spiegel* about fifteen years ago. It was his explanation of what we were doing in those days. The interview was about Kundera and Dreyfus but it was after the Germans caught a neo-Nazi mental patient wanting to kill Douglas, in Stuttgart. But he talked about his NYU life, for some reason. He talked about what he called Abstract Comedy. Abstract must mean not funny. We were young, of course."

"I was never told about this interview," Ned said.

"It's in German."

"So let's forget it," Ned said.

"Forget it," Iva said.

"We could be a panel," Gruen said. "Reminisce."

Elliot raised his voice. In his official tone, he said, "This is important. It has to be done right. There is a German foundation involved . . ."

Gruen broke in. "Wait I remember what Douglas said he wanted when he died."

"Stop interrupting," Elliot said.

"But this is what he said. He wished if we all outlived him we would go to some park and hide in the trees and when somebody came by we would shout *Great Pan is dead.* He *said* that."

Joris groaned. Iva looked at Gruen coldly. Nina whispered to Ned, "He thought quite highly of himself." Elliot heard this. He pressed his hair down with both hands and said something about coming to talk to them one at a time that night, late, or tomorrow.

The last course arrived. Nina murmured to Ned, "Oh. A dessert *trolley.*"

25 It was pouring again. Ned batted at the strings of rainwater trailing from the bulky cornice above the front door.

They were waiting for a wheelbarrow to be brought to them so they could go down to the cabin and transfer their belongings to the new room in the manse. The scene before them had changed a little. A substantial white trailer had appeared down the lawn, off to the side. A lit-up sandwich sign set up next to it said Serv-U. Flashlight beams swung in the darkness.

A young black man in a Serv-U uniform—yellow jumpsuit, knee-high yellow rubber boots—was accompanying Gruen and Joris to the tower to help in their relocation. Another of the Serv-U men ran up and abandoned a wheelbarrow directly in front of Ned and Nina, saying nothing. He hurried away. He had been an old black man with one milk-white eye, wearing a drenched watch cap. Serv-U was probably one of the minimum-wage day-labor outfits that raked up workers from among the homeless and unemployed in Kingston, which was richly supplied with them. He and Nina seemed to be on their own. Nina would hold up the golf umbrella while Ned pushed the wheelbarrow. They set off.

As they were turning the corner of the manse, Nina told Ned to stop. He was confused.

"Wait," she said sharply, startling him. Gesturing unclearly, she led him to a spot close to the house and pointed upward at a deck two floors above.

She spoke into his ear but she was too close. He pushed her away and quietly asked her to say it again so he could understand.

She said, "There's a traveling fight going on. You don't pay attention! It started back in the middle of the house and now it's here." One of the sliding doors leading to the deck was in play. It had been slammed shut and then opened and slammed shut again.

Iva and Elliot were fighting. Elliot was better than Iva at keeping his voice under control. She was in a volcanic state, threatening to call someone, apparently weeping. One of the two of them made a sound closer to a growl than Ned had ever heard anyone make.

"I *shall* talk to him, and he *will* come." That was Iva.

"Pressure him, and not only will he not come, he won't even send the video." That was Elliot. It was very intelligible. Something that sounded like rough body contact, or someone falling, was happening now. Then the traveling fight evidently moved off into other venues in the house. A voice distantly yelling was Iva's. Ned was holding his breath.

"I have no idea what this is," Ned said.

"I do," Nina said.

"You just got here," Ned said.

"Somebody important is not coming."

"I guess," Ned said, "that would be Kundera not coming."

"They're upset. And Dreyfus won't be coming either," Nina said.

"That's not funny," Ned said.

"Don't be an idiot," she said, and strode off with the umbrella. He followed. Over his shoulder he could see that Serv-U workers were unspooling electric lines from the trailer to the tower and the manse. It looked as though they were going to be around for a while.

The Serv-U worker with the white eye crossed their path. Where was Dale Coy, now? Ned wondered. He hadn't thought about him in years.

"For about six months," Ned said, "there was a black guy named Dale in our group, freshman year."

"He left the group?"

"He did."

"Why?"

"I don't remember," Ned said. But he did remember. He thought, Coy hated one of Douglas's Christmastime song parodies like "It's Beginning to Look a Bit Like Kwanzaa," and Doug hadn't spared the substitute Christmas promoted by Ron Karenga and the black nationalists in those days. But Douglas had done parodies of regular Christmas carols, too, lots of them. Ned thought, You can't call everything that's funny, funny, without losing friends.

He said, "We weren't that enlightened about race. I guess we assumed that bad race incidents were destined to be like firecracker explosions after the Fourth of July. They'd get fewer and fewer and then stop."

"I think that old man had a bleeding cut on his hand. There was blood on the wheelbarrow handle. None of them are wearing work gloves. It's cold, too."

"I could say something," Ned said.

"I'll remind you," she said.

26 Nina was out in the rain again, with her umbrella, standing near the hump of rock she and Ned had been calling Moby Dick, and she was there because it was one of the few places she was sure of getting a good cell phone connection.

Her mother answered. It would be about seven p.m. there.

"Okay tell me," her mother said.

"Everything's okay. Everything's working. I got here and nobody seems to mind."

"Where are you staying? What kind of place have they got you in?"

"Well we were in a sort of dollhouse, which I liked, but now we're moving to a new place in the main house. I just had a look at it. It's a nice room, pretty big, like a good motel room, everything you need, except we have to share a bathroom with Ned's friends Gruen and Joris. They're in the bedroom next to ours. It's a good big bed, and the room is built over a rollicking stream pretty much like Niagara Falls. Directly underneath us."

"*Oh that's so good*, Neen!" Her mother's sudden enthusiasm puzzled her. But that was Ma.

"Why is it, especially?"

"Negative ions, don't you know anything? It's good for theum . . . negative ions are pouring up from the mashing water."

"Okay."

"You pay plenty to get a negative ion generator, a machine. You're getting it free."

"Do I have to inhale a lot perchance?"

"*No*. It penetrates by itself. You'll wake up tomorrow and you'll feel wonderful, like running around, and Ned too."

"Good. He needs a lift. By the way, we did it on time."

"Thank God then."

"And Ma, listen. I think that a couple of hours afterward I felt something new like a very refined I don't mean refined I mean fine, as in . . . fine thing like a . . . fizzing, in there. I feel it right now."

"Okay, I'm going to go out on a plank and say you did it."

She wanted to believe Ma. It was sad, but she wanted

her to be right. Her mother had called herself a dialectical materialist until she decided to learn astrology, which wasn't a good fact to be thinking about now.

Nina said, "I hope you're right."

"I am. In your voice I hear something."

"You didn't used to believe things like this."

"I still don't. But I can do it. I got *attuned*. So listen to me for your own good. And by the way since you're being smart with me I'll tell you something else you have to do. You have to watch where you sleep from now on."

"Oh God, what does that mean?"

"It means you have to be head north feet south."

"Well if your head is north the only place your feet can be is south, right?"

"Okay, be smart with me. It's *alignment*. If you grow carrots in a tray of dirt and grow them *athwart* the axis you get crummy short carrots but if you align the dirt bed along the axis you get tall sweet ones. And don't laugh, this is in a decent book by a man René Dubos, an MD who was supported for years by that bloodsucker Rockefeller at the Rockefeller whatever it is medical foundation. So align your bed."

"I'll do my best. I'll take care of it."

"The march, howum," Ma said.

"We're still getting good news. How about you?"

"Don't worry about Los Angeles, but something is wrong, I can tell, you're not telling me."

Nina sighed. "I'm trying to think of what it might be."

Ma said, "You know."

"Well the only thing it might be is the son of Ned's friend who died, he's a peeping Tom. I know this because he peeped at me. He's fourteen or fifteen."

"I knew it," Ma said.

"Well, you didn't know *it*."

"You told Ned. Ned will take care of it. You be careful."

There was more from her mother about the LA march. Lots of unions were in. Stars were going to be in it. It was going to be bigger than the Tom Mooney demonstrations, whatever they were. I can't listen, Nina thought.

"The only other thing bothering me is that Ned's friends haven't signed his petition, and he cares."

Ma was outraged for Ned. "*What?* Why not? What kind of friends? Get *out* of that place then."

"I can't. We can't. There's one in particular he wants to sign. So Dear Abby here's my question: I could go behind Ned's back and beg this person, which is what it would come down to . . ."

Ma was emphatic against it. She said, "Absolutely not. You'd have to make him swear never to tell and then it would be a secret and it would be like rubble under the bottom sheet you could never get rid of . . ."

"Ma you just convinced me."

"How big a deal is it? I could run the cards. I know I know. But they help me think."

"No, I said you convinced me."

"You need to cheer him up. You know how. Get his mind off this."

Nina laughed. "I know what you're talking about but you don't know what you're talking about. I'm wearing him out in that department, poor guy. When we get through with this he won't want to come near my chocha for a year and a half. I can see it, *Get that thing out of here*, he'll say."

"You're right, because of theum. Okay so forget that."

"Okay, time to go, my cell is almost dead anyway. I have to go help Ned with our stuff."

"Call me anytime," Ma said.

There was an argument for trying to get some hijinks going here in the cabin rather than in their room in the manse. It was quiet and private in the cabin and it was mental up in the manse. There were interruptions. Ned was looking at her in a nice way. He had liked it earlier when she'd told him that the reason she'd first gotten interested in him was because he was so verbal looking. He had brightened up. But she had decided that easing up was the best idea.

Something was heating up Ned's confessional impulses.

Ned felt he should peel the paper off the windows before they left the place. She wanted to leave it to Serv-U. He wanted her to help him. It wouldn't take long. Ned uncovered the first pane and went rigid, staring out into the night. *She knew what it had to be.*

She ran to the cabin door, threw it open, and stepped out onto the little porch and shouted as commandingly as she could, "*Come here, you, Hume, you come here. Hume!*"

Don't do this, she was thinking. At the side of the house, it was Hume, rising. When he saw her coming at him, he lost his footing and fell back against the side of the building. She hesitated. She was going to arrest him! Where was Ned? She stood over the boy. "*You,*" she said. She pressed an open hand over her crotch, ridiculously, to protect herself there. Unhelpful rain blew into her face. She sensed that something was wrong with the boy. He'd surely had time to run. He was wearing the same odd leather ensemble as before and he was drenched. Ned arrived and pushed her aside. And then Ned was hauling the boy around to the porch. Hume wasn't resisting.

"*Don't be rough with him,*" Nina said. She resisted the impulse to take hold of Hume's clothing somewhere.

Hume and Ned stood apart from each other, and Ned, almost courteously, made an ushering gesture to the boy. They entered the cabin. Hume seemed to be limping. He had strong body odor.

Nina thought, How can this be? He was handsome and solid. He had a *cleft chin*, cut to just the right slight depth. He was a rugged boy with fine shoulders. He should be beleaguered with girlfriends following him around. He was as tall as Ned.

Hume was being compliant. Everything remained to be seen. Apparently she was the only one he would make eye contact with, for now. He was something like a fine animal, a fine horse, which was a stupid thought. Whoever had cut his hair was a criminal. The two cropped dark ridges running back were like dorsal fins. There were scabs and scratches in the shaved areas of his scalp. He wasn't taking care of himself. His eyes were maybe the best color for a man to have, a pale blue, which she thought of as a *bitter* color. He had accepted a seat on one of the kitchen chairs. Ned was sitting opposite him. There was no chair for her so she leaned against the wall.

How she could bring this into the discussion she had not the slightest idea, but she thought it might improve things for this kid if he could comprehend the bizarre image of a woman he'd stumbled in on, naked, upside down, legs stretched up the wall. She thought, This is the definition of hopeless.

Ned seemed uncertain. She knew what was happening—he had too much to say and he didn't want to start off with clichés. And he was sitting too close to Hume. It made it inquisitorial. So what she could do was go over and pull on the back of his chair a little. He would get the point. She did it and it worked.

Ned said, "I'm Ned and this is my wife Nina and I am an old, old friend of your father. And I, I want to say something to you: I'm really sorry."

Hume was rolling his right pant leg up, with difficulty because it was leather and it was wet. A grossly swollen ankle was emerging.

"*Okay,*" the boy shouted, stunning Ned with the violence of his delivery. Hume was picking bits of something off his flesh. Nina thought, You cannot run around over boulders in the rain in shoes like that. He was sockless, wearing what appeared to be espadrilles in the last stages of disintegration.

Ned stood up. "Why are you shouting at me? I mean God damn you anyway, Hume, you know what you did this afternoon, God damn you . . ."

Nina took Ned by the arm. Ned was shaking. Nina mouthed the word Stop.

Ned wouldn't. "Now God damn it, you violated my wife's privacy. Who are you? Why do you think you can do that? You can go to jail for that . . ."

Nina said, "*Hume,* nobody knows about it. We haven't told anyone."

"I'm sorry I looked at you," Hume said, slowly, in a tone that seemed to deny what he was saying.

Ned detected slyness and couldn't control himself. "Now God damn you *again*. Listen, what is going on with you? What are you doing besides running around in the woods, for Christ's sake?"

She thought, I hate it here, the whole fucking area: it's dank and I hate the boring trees and the towns are decrepit . . . and peculiar without being in any way picturesque . . . somebody said that about someplace. In Kingston she had seen the ghost of a nineteenth-century sign on the side of a brick building in white letters barely legible, CORSETERIA.

"What about your mother?" Ned asked Hume harshly.

"What about her?" Hume answered.

"Your mother was devastated—is, I mean. Why aren't you helping her?"

"She wants me to leave," Hume said.

"What does *that* mean?"

Hume said, "She does. You don't know anything about my mother."

"And that's all you have to say about spying on my wife?"

"Sorry. Apologize." The sly tint would not leave his voice.

Ned said, "What does your father mean to you, nothing? I want to know. Was he not a good father to you?"

"You don't *know* anything. My mother is stupid."

Nina bent over Hume and took him by the shoulders. She said, "If you want to be a monster, be one, but now you have to come up to the house and let somebody take care of your ankle. How did you do that?"

"Crossing the creek."

"I knew it," she said, looking meaningfully at Ned. "I told you it was dangerous."

Nina wanted to give ibuprofen to Hume. She had some

in her purse, which was atop the load of their belongings in the wheelbarrow parked on the corner of the porch. She went to get it.

Hume was following her movements and was already shaking his head. She brought a glass of water from the kitchen and tried to hand it to him along with two pills. He rolled his eyes. She rolled hers.

"Now we'll go up the hill," Ned said.

It was tense. Ned tried to support Hume, who said that no one should touch him. They let him go on ahead, limping.

"I was completely ineffective," Ned said quietly to Nina.

"No you were not. But anyway, so was I."

"It wasn't up to you, it was up to me."

She thought, Oh you poor man. He was concluding that he had failed as a father, that it had been a tryout, and he had failed to, what would you call it, improve on Douglas as a father, who had clearly been a dud and miserable at it.

"Now where is he going?" Ned asked. Hume had broken away, taking a path that would lead him around the back of the manse and presumably to some entrance not known to them. There had been no goodbye, unsurprisingly.

Nina said, "You know what you're doing—you're chain-sighing, a thing you accuse me of. You make me stop doing that, so you stop. It's noticeable."

Hume was gone and she was glad he was gone. She was going to relax now. They had said what they had to say. She was sorry for men. She pitied Hume. Puberty is torture, she thought, depending on where you are when it happens, and who's around. Ned was sad.

27 "Where's your better half?" Joris asked Ned.

"Interior decorating. Rearranging the deck chairs." Ned looked around the bedroom assigned to Gruen and Joris. "Your digs are identical to ours."

"Same nice big bed. We have to sleep together, like you guys. Head to toe because I don't want his cold," Joris said, pointing at Gruen, who said, "I don't want it either."

Ned sat down in an armchair at the foot of the bed. His two friends were lying on the bed a yard apart, under the spread, drinking, their heads on pillows propped directly against the glass of the great window looking into blackness. The rumbling brook below was a presence in the dull room. This wing of four rooms was cantilevered directly over it. There was no reading lamp, only an amber fixture in the ceiling shedding the sort of light he associated with hotel corridors.

Gruen said, "You know I bet those people who lived in what was it called, yeah, the Falling Waters House Frank Lloyd Wright built them moved out in about six months. It was just like this place. I can see the wife saying *I'm going mad I tell you, mad.*"

"Where did you get the sambuca?" Ned asked. There was a liter bottle of sambuca two-thirds full on the floor next to Joris. They were drinking from paper cups.

"We stole it," Gruen and Joris said in unison.

Joris said, "And you can't have any. Yes you can."

"No thanks," Ned said.

"Right now we're lounging," Gruen said.

"We like it," Joris said.

Gruen gestured vehemently for Ned to lock the door to the room, or at least that's what the rotary motions of his right hand seemed to mean.

Ned got up, turned the lock, and resumed his seat.

He said, "For your information, if you don't aim your bed north/south you're going to turn into a stunted carrot. Or something. Because you're thwarting the earth energies that make you big and strong. I just moved our bed."

"Beg pardon?" Gruen said.

"Nina gets these things from an advanced thinker, her mother. Nina doesn't believe them but I have to execute anyway."

Gruen said, "Joris is in the middle of something that will make your hair stand on end. His life in the whore world. He doesn't care. He is fucking telling all about it. It's the best fucking story you ever heard. And we don't want any interruptions."

"Jesus, what have I missed?" Ned said.

Joris said, "You missed when I was telling about when I first became a whoremonger . . ."

Ned said, "Well wait a minute. A fishmonger is somebody who sells fish, isn't it?"

"Oh shut up," Gruen said.

Joris said, "I have to say this for Douglas. He did make me think behind words. But on that one if you look in the OED you'll find that a whoremonger is somebody just like me, who *goes* to whores. I'll tell you, a pretty amazing moment was when I figured out that *your highness* meant your way-up-aboveness in physical space and nothing else. Also Douglas pointed out that revolution doesn't mean the most pissed-on rising to the top forever, it means one more turn of the wheel, turn the crank and revolve the oppressors. Also *exclusive* neighborhoods is funny. It means exclude poor smelly bastards . . . and *very exclusive* neighborhoods means exclude *more* of them. And the *most* exclusive neighborhoods means exclude *all* of them."

They were all silent for a while, giving Douglas credit, Ned understood.

"I decided I had to go to a therapist to find out what it was with me and married women and also to see if one would have anything persuasive against the way I was going to whores. I was liking it. I mean, it made me happy. The first shrink I went to seemed a little too interested in making me get married again. He's divorced now."

Weirdly, Gruen sang out, in a clear voice, "Tournent, tournent, mes personnages . . ." and then stopped. Joris repeated it. That was the intro music from supposedly the greatest movie of all time, *La Ronde*. They'd seen it three times at Douglas's insistence, to get its essence.

There was more about the brothel world that Joris inhabited. Ned tried not to feel sordid at the close attention he was paying and he thought it made him look bad to ask for elucidations so he didn't. There were nineteen women in an extremely comfortable six-bedroom apartment on the Upper West Side. There was turnover, but not substantial, and some of the women were permanent fixtures and had developed long-term relationships with certain men. It was all middle class, clean, the madam was a wonderful cook. If a girl used drugs she was through. Two doctors were clients. They supervised the health of the women, who accepted the protocol that spot checks for either drugs or STDs would happen at random times.

Joris's narrative was a lumpy arc. He was going back repeating some things he'd already described to Gruen. He was saying that he'd never gotten to the bottom of his fetish, if that was what it was, for other men's wives. And he was saying that he couldn't tell anyone about his personal life, because he had no friends. He had business associates but no friends. He had acquaintances but no friends. And he said that probably the nature of his personal life made him wary about the idea of friends. He didn't know.

Gruen said, "Wait. I have no friends either!"

Ned laughed. "It doesn't seem to bother you that much."

Gruen drained his cup and said, "I don't think it does. I'm busy."

Now Joris was going back over his preliminary study of the whorehouse possibilities in Manhattan. Ned didn't need to be convinced that every variety of sexual taste would find its supplier in a big city and he was already convinced that there was no accounting for tastes. He was glad that Joris had found a comfortable bordello.

Everything that Joris had to say about whores was fascinating. There was a whole lore there, no rhyme intended. Gruen was maintaining himself in an abnormally still state lest any inadvertent move derail Joris's revelations. The brothel women, the older ones, naturally, resented the pressure to *present young*, as they called it, and they particularly disliked the whole new waxing imperative. The pressure went beyond that. There were mothers among the women, and more of them were getting half-zips, vaginal tightening. On the other hand, there was an older john constituency for natural escutcheons, the bigger and thicker the better, and some felt uncomfortable or self-conscious with partners so much younger than they were, and chose the oldest of the women. And there was a new house specialty, participatory labial shaving, that some johns were willing to pay a premium for. Condoms were mandatory. Joris swore that he had never had an STD. It was collegial in the brothel, although there was some rivalry, Joris had to admit, over his attentions. There were four or five women who were very happy to see Joris step into the place. He had accommodations at the brothel, minimal, to use when he felt like it—a bed and informal office space. He dispensed legal advice gratis from time to time, helpful to them despite the fact that they were not seagoing vessels. The talent, which was what Joris sometimes referred to the women as, used diaphragms to prevent bleeding when they had their periods. His wife had done that, too. And so had Nina, Ned thought. Men had their preferences. An occasional one was for the talent to put on eyeglasses, and there was one client who paid extra, now and then, to have any of the women who were free come into the room he was using and applaud as he approached his orgasm. There would be cheers and gratuities all around.

Joris fell silent. They waited. The trace of foreignness in his speech was still there, but faint. Ned remembered telling Joris *I said to me* was impossible English in probably the first week of their friendship. No one could claim they hadn't all been helpful to one another.

Gruen was fumbling around distractingly under the spread. Intoning, he said, "A man, a plan . . . a banana," and pulled one out from the bedclothes.

Joris helped himself to more sambuca. He was having a contemplative interlude. It ended. "I live in pain," he said, in a flat tone. He followed the words with a smile, obviously meant to be rueful but registering with Ned as desperate.

Cancer, Ned thought. He sat up in his chair, rigid. Gruen violently reorganized the pillows behind his head so that he could turn on his side and look straight at Joris more easily.

Ned said, "What do you mean?"

"It's not medical. Relax," Joris said.

"Thank Christ," Ned said. So then it would be depression.

Joris said, "And also it's not depression. I am not depressed and I tell you absolutely there's nothing a shrink could do. It's not all the time. It's like this, it's like an insect sound that comes up when I think about my life. My life so far. And the insect sound has pain connected to it. It's like tinnitus that hurts when I consider certain things . . ."

Ned said, "I thought it was going to be cancer. Jesus. It does sound like depression to me, actually . . ."

Joris said, "I thought it wouldn't come when I got here. Don't ask me why. But."

Gruen said, "Remorse, it sounds like to me."

"For *what*?" Ned said, irritated.

Gruen was ahead of Joris in the sambuca department and the result was that pretty soon everything he had to contribute would be a non sequitur. Ned could see that coming, Gruen turning into an impediment. It was something that happened when Gruen drank.

Joris said, "The truth is I have nothing to complain about. My sons are okay, and they're good very good to their mother."

"Then *don't* complain," Gruen said.

Oh no, Ned thought. Drink also brought out a censorious side of Gruen. It was an odd thing. It was contrary to the normal Gruen.

Gruen said, "It's remorse, it sounds like."

"You said that. *What* is?" Joris said.

"The way you feel that you were just complaining about."

"What's your point, if there is one?" Joris was getting angry.

Gruen said, "Okay, you go to whores and it's friendly but underneath they are doing it with you against their real wishes . . . That's whoring. They do it with people they might reject in a free state of mind. I'm not saying anything you don't know."

This was wrong, Ned thought. Joris had arrived at some kind of personal adaptation to a problem, an unfortunate fetish for married women, and it was working, and his friends should support him. It was simple.

"Wait a second," Ned said. "It's not your business. You get paid for what you do and you don't only do what you would do for free. And it's working for Joris, and it's presumably working for the women who're happy to see him show up at the door."

Beyond that, Ned didn't know what to say. Douglas's death was bound to bring out all the anxieties that go with looking back and summing up what a life came down to, the choices made, what the verdict would be if life ended suddenly without any warning or chance to do the things that were left to do that could improve the judgment an existence got. That was the downside of sudden death. *A* downside, he meant. But the moods Joris was talking about had been going on long before Douglas died.

Gruen was not through with Joris. Ned could tell

because Gruen was running his tongue over his upper teeth. That meant he was about to say something important. It went with alcohol.

Ned wasn't satisfied with what he himself had said, so far. There seemed to be no place to go with Joris's declaration, his confession. Joris had trusted them.

Gruen said, "I'm sorry. I can be wrong. In fact I am. So I'm sorry."

Ned thought, It's too late.

Joris said to Gruen, "Thank you, David."

Ned thought, I wish Joris could just be *for* something. Or against it . . . how pointless of me, but it could be the Anglo-Saxon Invasion, if he would let it.

Ned said, "We all have our dark moments." In some dark moments—visited by sins of omission, *mistakes* . . . Ned would say aloud, *Mutual Aid*. It was a trick. Ostensibly he was reminding himself of a classic he had pledged to read years ago, and hadn't. It was a trick that in a disguised way acknowledged the stab of regret and in the same breath knocked it away. *What Is to Be Done?* was another title he used. Nina had figured it all out, of course.

What the friends needed was to be back at the round clawfoot table in their Second Avenue place, everybody sitting up alert, a decanter of red wine on the table, somebody saying *This is the issue before us*, bringing his fist down like a gavel, Elliot usually, or Douglas, or he himself, often enough.

They were in a conversational eddy. Gruen had gotten out of bed, dispensed with the sweater he'd been wearing, and begun to stalk aimlessly around the room in his boxers. Ned thought, Man I love you but you need a regimen. Between sips of sambuca Gruen seemed to be free-associating about his wife, Helen, more to himself than for the benefit of the group. He was proceeding as though it was his turn to talk about his intimate life. If they think I'm going next after Gruen in this area, they can forget it, Ned thought.

Gruen's disclosures were on the pastel side, after Joris's. Helen always wanted certain music on during sex and Gruen had to have just gotten out of the shower and he had to be sure to remember to see that his nails were groomed. His wife always wore a negligee for the occasion. He couldn't complain. She had to sort of elevate the thing in order to let go, for some reason. It didn't matter. She put her heart into it. She was taking a plunge, each time. For her it was like going off a dive tower.

"You have to give her credit," Gruen said, wanly.

"We do," Joris said, which was a peculiar thing to say. But then what *Gruen* had said was peculiar, seeming as it did to take the position that his wife deserved credit for having sex. Ned thought, You can ask about certain facts of life but not others. And evidently that was all Gruen had to say for the moment.

And Joris was dormant. In fact, both of them were looking expectantly in Ned's direction. I love group dynamics, Ned thought. The body language directed at him was saying he should now give them the minutiae about Claire. He didn't want to. He would tell what he had to.

Joris startled him by saying, "I loved Claire. And then I hated Claire. Watch me speak freely on this. When in the future history of the world I am ever going to find a group of people interested in my opinions on this subject is never. So here's the truth. She was a shit. With all respect, because

I know you got together with her on the coast and then you were together for those years, she was no good. And she was so pale I always wanted to buy her a steak. Douglas was her tool. She made little things disappear. When she came into the room everybody had to try to ignore her beauty so anything separate from her could get done, which she knew. And she wasn't a nice person. She was passive. She was so passive that anything anybody proposed that didn't work out was somebody else's fault. She was the one who got us banned from the Alliance Française. I forget what she did . . ."

For Ned, there was shock to digest. It was a subject that could trap him into ugliness in what he said. But he had to say something. He thought he knew where to go. He said, "I'm not going to say anything about Claire, really. Although it's interesting to hear that she had itchy fingers even back then. You know we connected over a shoplifting incident when I was at Pacific Co-op for a while and then lo and behold. This was three or four years after NYU. Gruen knows about it already. A clerk caught her shoplifting. I took care of it and that's how it started up with us. A Nation of Shoplifters, somebody said back then . . ."

Suddenly he knew clearly where to take this. The problem with going into detail about Claire was that it made him look like a fool and a dupe. He didn't want to revisit any of it, and Joris's contribution had made the picture even worse. So he was going to talk about Nina. They knew nothing about Nina.

"Now Nina, you could say Nina contains multitudes. I'll just tell you about this because it sheds light on certain aspects of my girl. You don't know anything about her yet, of course. You will. But here's something she wouldn't tell you. She's a terrible sleeper. She starts getting night thoughts the minute she lies down. For example, we're trying to get pregnant. So she worries about that. She can't read herself to sleep because she gets too interested. Did I mention that she has too many interests? So she needs some kind of custom distraction to help her get to sleep. She has to get up at six thirty for work. Movies are out because even a completely crap narrative holds her attention. We tried some judge shows but she kept kibitzing the cases and soliciting my views. So then we discovered thank God ValueVision. The jewelry shows especially. It's endless pitching by dressed-up women. Prodigies who can talk for thirty minutes about a fucking ring! About twenty minutes of focusing on the words bores her to sleep. The timer turns it off automatically. The funny thing is, it puts me to sleep, too. I recommend it. I've even learned things I never knew existed from it—drusy, bale, bezel, station necklace, and so on. Did you know that zircon is a real stone, I mean *gem*stone, and not a diamond simulant? Ever hear of a diamond simulant? And do you know what the second most cavernous state in America is? Missouri. They have over seven thousand registered caverns. Did you even know they *registered* caverns? Anyway, she, we, developed a comedy regimen around this sideshow. We renamed the models and the presenters and the experts. The names have to be apt. One woman who has an unidentifiable accent is Foreigna. A kind of slutty model is Traila. One woman is Wigga. Sometimes I come up with completely good names she won't let me use because they're unkind. She has veto power. I wanted to name a plus-sized model Ponderosa, but she said no. Also no to Refrigerata . . ."

"I *get* it," Joris said. Gruen laughed.

A bout of knocking shook the door. Gruen got back under the covers. Ned went to the door and opened it, and Nina, furious about something, stood there. She strode into the room.

There was no preamble. "*Forgive me*, but God damn it, you guys, these two rooms are sharing the same bathroom and I am not going to step in your spillage in my bare feet. I don't know you that well."

Ned said, "We're sorry, Nina. We—"

"I doubt it's you," she said to Ned.

"He's toilet trained," Gruen said, not taking it seriously enough for Nina, who turned on him.

She pointed at Gruen as she continued. "This is what you do, and please do it for eternity. It goes like this. You unzip, raise the seat, and address the toilet from *above*, as follows. You take your unit out and you *straddle* the toilet, which yes you *can* do without pushing your pants down. You lean slightly forward toward the wall behind the tank. You aim straight down like your stream is an *Olympic diver* going down *straight*. You shake any drops on your unit off *over the bowl*. Don't *hurry* before you step back. And this is the most important thing your mother never told you—and it's *rehouse your thing while it's still over the bowl*. And then check around and if you've spilled anything, you clean it up yourself and then you leave. It's *easy*."

The men were rattled.

Nina backed out of the room, closing the door softly.

Again Gruen had his head under the covers.

He emerged, asking if she was gone yet.

"Good for her," Joris said.

Ned was proud.

28 Ned stood in the corridor. He wanted to look at his notebook before he joined Nina in the bedroom. She was always curious about his jottings but sometimes he didn't want to be asked about them. He could be as asinine as the next man, in his reminders and creations.

The top page in his little notebook read:

For Eulogy—METAPHOR

— Life a gigantic auditorium in which a play that never ends is in progress.
— Everything is dark, the seats, everything except the stage. People arrive in the theater.—One stream of personae goes straight to the seating. The other lines up in front of a Takacheck machine which is distributing parts to play.
— Ultimately the Takacheck people end up on stage.
— The theater is haunted by an immortal invisible sniper who strikes whenever he feels like it. Nothing can be done about him. He kills actors, concentrating on the older ones, but not exclusively.
— The dead are taken out one by one. New actors join the cast. The sniper kills members of the audience as well.
— This metaphor is useless.

He tore the page out and rolled it into a pellet he had no idea what to do with. He flicked it down the hall. Then he retrieved it and dropped it into his pocket for flushing later.

29 They were getting ready for bed, at last. She needed more sleep than she was likely to get in the next few days, but the problem was that around there it was like a novel. There were white spaces on the map of the relationships she was poring over.

Ned was undressing. She expected him to say something about her underpants. He didn't like the cut and he didn't like the material and he called them grandma pants. When he comes back from flossing watch him say something, she thought.

"May I say something about your unmentionables?" Ned asked.

She was beginning to hate friendship. He was mixing up friendship with acts and atmospheres from the deluded matrix the boys had lived in for a heartbeat in the seventies. She thought, *I* am your friend, you idiot, and I let you into my perfect body, for Christ's sake. "Why do you hate plaid so much, do you know?" Nina asked.

"I just don't like it."

"And why do you hate the word '*valid*,' would you say?"

"Because people use valid when they're too chicken to say whether something being asserted is true or false."

"Oh bullshit! People may misuse it but you can just as well apply it to a piece of evidence or reasoning offered in a debate. And why would you bother to have an attitude about people who say 'feisty' or 'meld' or 'vibrant'? Only because Douglas did, am I right? And now you can tell me if Douglas happened to have a special opinion about plaid."

Ned thought about it. "Okay he did."

"Based on *what*?"

"I can't remember."

She threw herself into the bed. She wanted to lie still for a while. A thing she liked about the permanent delicate subliminal trembling of the room caused by the pounding torrents below was that it kept her from dowsing for occult signals from her uterus.

Ned joined her under the blankets, saying, "I have come here directly from the tent pole factory."

Nina woke Ned with an incomprehensible message in his ear. The room was black. Gently he pushed her head away from his and said, "Say it again." He pressed the crown of his wristwatch, which illuminated the dial. They had been asleep for just two hours.

"Something is waking me up," Nina said.

"Me too."

"Two things are. Listen. There's something going on. In the hall. Knocking and whispering. Why don't you go out there and look around?"

"Because I don't feel like it and I don't want to know what's going on, I don't care."

"Don't get grumbly," she said.

"Oh for God's sake," he said. "I don't want to know what's going on and I don't need another task. I could be on the phone all day tomorrow trying to find out what's going on with the *Convergence,* you think I need another task? You're making *me* get the names of all the help in the place so *you* can greet them the way you want to, for God's sake, and the staff is multiplying as we speak instead of sleeping."

"Multiplying like coat hangers. That's what Ma used to say."

"Well Ma hit the nail on the head with that one. Nina, please be quiet."

She observed a pause, then said, "There are no curtains in here you know. And that peeping Tom son of your best friend is still on the loose."

He exploded at her. "God damn it! He would have to be a lizard to get his head outside our window, not to mention that Niagara Falls is down there."

She was silent for a while, again. The hallway was still. But she was annoyed. She was wishing she'd put on her plaid underpants and gone out in the hall that way. No doubt they all hated plaid.

Now she was remembering something she'd forgotten she did. She'd made a note to herself after the last call to her mother. She tapped Ned on the shoulder.

"*What?*" he asked.

"I think we're being unfair to my mother too much. Do you know what the Akashic Record is?"

"No, but you're going to tell me. Help."

"I'll be brief. It was one of her beliefs, okay? It was the theosophical idea that every thought you have gets recorded out in the ether in this thing called the Akashic Record. So I said to her, That's the most fascist thing I ever heard of. How can anyone live with that? I must have been about twelve or thirteen and all I had to say was *fascist* and she dropped it immediately. I'd said the magic word. I give her credit."

"Wonderful," he said. He pushed the covers down preparatory to getting up for a trip to the bathroom. They slept naked, which was unlike the nighttime protocols under Claire.

Nina turned her penlight on his penis. "Handsome penis," Nina said, and then said, "These are pretty, too," brushing her naked breasts with the beam of the penlight.

"Don't be relentless," he said.

He was right. They needed their sleep.

30 Nina was sleeping in. Yet somehow she had tasked him with the mission of finding yogurt for her somewhere. He'd forgotten to ask if he was supposed to wake her up when he found it, if he did find it. The fact that she'd had a sudden sharp food preference could be good news.

So far he had asked two obviously wrong people if there was any yogurt they knew of. The ground floor was overrun with media. They were around every corner. The kitchen was a chaos. Calling the media people ninjas had started with Joris. It was appropriate because they were all similarly dressed in dark clothing and were always disconcertingly darting about. They came and went, came and went, communing with one another in European languages, German mainly. Elliot had instructed the friends not to interact with the media.

Ned had his petitions with him, arranged with the top blank petition just askew enough to show that it rested on a thick block of filled-up petition forms. That was show business. There were blank petition forms at the bottom of the block. Nina had gotten on his case about the petitions. She was accusing him of mixing up the question of self-worth with getting all the friends to sign. He had denied it, knowing it was true, and she had said, I'm thinking of writing your biography and I have a good title for it, but unfortunately it's been used, and he'd said, Okay, what? and she'd said, *The Neurotic Personality of Our Time*, you poor thing. He understood everything. She'd said she wanted him to keep his spirits up so he could keep her spirits up for the sake of their, as she was already calling it, their homunculus.

Ned went out the front door to look at the scene developing all over the place. Elliot was trotting up the drive, followed by a ninja.

Ned ran up to Elliot, who declined to stop, so Ned fell in beside him, all the way into the living room where Ned was inspired to hold his clipboard out in a way that blocked Elliot's viewfield. Elliot stopped and so did the ninja.

"My petition, Elliot. It's against . . ."

"I know what it's against. I don't need to sign that."

"What do you mean?" And this is my friend Elliot, Ned thought.

Elliot said, "I have no time to explain this now. Look around. But Ned there isn't going to be a war."

"What do you *mean*?"

"What we're doing is called compellence. *Compellence*. It's a bluff."

"So you think he'll just leave, Hussein?"

"He will. He'll join Idi Amin someplace nice. Riyadh. I have to get to the office."

"You don't understand," Ned said.

"*You* don't," Elliot said. What he was insinuating was that he, Elliot, was operating at a loftier level of contacts and information and should be left alone by Ned.

Ned thought, At least he looks uncomfortable doing that. He said, straining for a neutral tone, "I'll talk to you later."

"Good! At the seminar."

"What seminar? Do you mean the planning session for the memorial?"

"That's it."

31 Ned found Gruen in the physic garden. Gruen was just putting his cell phone away, in his jacket pocket. He looked yellow. He said, "Never again, sambuca."

"I thought we learned never to get drunk on liqueur," Ned said.

"You should have reminded me. By the way, right here is good for phoning. Better than down by that rock, and closer." Gruen shook himself. He said, "I missed breakfast, but a woman named Nadine Rose, I can describe her, dug up a container of yogurt for me. Now, Nadine Rose, her job is, as it was explained to me, is to fix you up with any kind of food you need between meals. She's Jamaican. She's the extremely pretty one, maybe thirty. For some reason she told me she was single. I didn't ask. Nadine Rose."

Ned held out his petitions to Gruen. Gruen sighed and said no.

And then it was exactly what Ned had anticipated. Gruen was sure Saddam Hussein was developing nuclear weapons because he had done it before. And the Israelis had blown up the Osirak reactor and his recollection was that Ned had been fine with that years ago despite the fact that it was plainly illegal under international law, the same way the invasion of Iraq in the next couple of months was going to be, unfortunately.

Ned said, "But the scale of this is going to be completely different. This is not going to be about killing seven French technicians." Ned faltered. There were too many factors that had to be left below the surface when it came to Israel. The main one was the rightness or wrongness of asserting a right to have a state dedicated to one religion only. It was hard to be fair, very hard. And another problem was the general demographic apocalypse that Jews worldwide were facing through assimilation and low birth rates, which made it all the more urgent to get rid of the criminals who were going out of their way to speed up that process through terror, by terrorizing Israel. Ned had his own dubious solution for the Arab-Israeli problem. It was to let America be the homeland for all Jews, any Jews, from anywhere, right of return, and let the UN take over all the holy sites for Jews and Islamics alike over there. Then the world would see what the Arabs did with the place. It had no oil and the Dead Sea was evaporating.

Ned said, "Gruen, do you really believe he has nuclear weapons?"

Gruen had something green in his mouth. He had plucked mint leaves from a bush growing in the ruined garden.

Ned was encouraged by Gruen's delay in replying, and said, "War isn't the only way. If we can convince Bush that there is going to be so much unhappiness in this country, you'll be surprised at how fast he comes up with, oh, boycotts, seizures of assets, blowing up the ports maybe, which I could go for, I suppose, but if there's an invasion? How much blood is going to be spilled are you thinking? And for *how long*? And one other thing. You *want* to sign this because I can tell you we are going to have *millions* of people in the streets, not thousands *millions*. Douglas would sign this petition but he's dead."

Gruen's smile was a truly beautiful thing, it had to be said.

He signed.

Ned said, "Now for Joris. But first Nadine Rose."

He had to get Joris out of the way. A Nadine Rose did exist, but her whereabouts were a mystery. No one in the kitchen at present had ever heard of yogurt, to judge by their mystified expressions when he used the word. Most of them had to be emergency hires who understandably felt no urgency to assist him in his quest. He wondered if he was signaling to them that he could safely be ignored. Ah well, he thought.

A glowing sun room lay ahead of him, down a dim corridor. He had walked through the sun room a couple of times. Ned was certain, for no good reason, that he would find Joris there.

Blinking, he entered the brightness. The air was tepid and humid. The room was solid glass on three sides. Thriving ferns stood in copper planters along the window walls, some growing so tall they would block the vista in places for anyone sitting down. He found Joris in an oversized rattan armchair, hunched over an enviable leatherbound notebook. The chairback fanned up and out so flamboyantly that from the rear Joris had been invisible. Ned sat down next to him in a matching chair. Joris closed the notebook. His feet were resting on a grisly thing Ned hoped was one of those ingenious resin replicas the Chinese produced in every branch of home décor. It was an elephant-foot ottoman with a metal cap on top. Joris looked at Ned with his eyebrows raised in question, but his attitude was friendly enough. He waved away Ned's apology for interrupting. Ned gripped his clipboard. The elephant foot was real, he could tell. A musty smell in the immediate vicinity that he was surely imagining seemed to be emanating from the thing.

Joris put his hand on the block of petition forms. He said, "I know what you want and I wish I could make you happy and sign that. Also, your wife. She is nice as they come and I wish I could add to her happiness. I don't know if you know that she asked me just lightly had you gotten hold of me yet with this petition to sign. Not asking me directly but putting a nice kind of pressure. I didn't mind."

An odd thing was that Ned felt himself looking forward to the contest that was coming. And if he could have sciencefictionally gotten Nina out of bed, into and out of the shower, dressed her and fed her, all in sixty seconds so that she could come and watch them fight, he would have done it.

Joris said, "But here's what: *they are going to do it*, whatever you do. The government decides what it wants. The State sings the Song of the State. Brecht, I believe. The Congress is out of it. And war makes money for the happy few. War is like the prime interest rate, it is something the government takes care of. Or like the Geodetic Survey, it is something the government takes care of. The people don't care. There's no draft.

"And you know what? I bet they love it. The government loves it that you put on big walks and demonstrations, as big as hell, and you know why? Why is because it keeps up the lie that you can do something about it, that the government can be touched in its heart. And wars don't lose you elections, either. When the draft was on it was a little bit different, but not now. And don't forget *they lie.* And you can't prove it's a lie until thirty years later a scholar might and by then nobody cares.

"Okay, so all that is under the heading on one side called Wasting Your Time. So now, come to the heading of killing as a good idea or not. Wait, first just to remind you . . . the reason Finland never went communist in 1918 to 1920 is because the government had a pogrom against the communists living there, thousands of them, trade unions, schools, everything, the White Terror, they called that massacre, and today Finland is a sturdy good little democracy, a place you could live in by choice, and they manufacture the piece-of-shit phone I use.

"So here is what it is . . ."

Ned said, "Soon you'll let me respond!"

Joris said, "I shall! As God is my witness, your voice shall sound! But here is what it is. These people we are supposed to go over and kill?—we *helped* them be stupid. We *subsidized* their insane religion all over south Asia, *us,* we gave guns to the Wahabis, and money. We don't like what we made but somebody has to kill it and in my opinion it's the least we can do."

Ned said, "May I . . . ?"

"*Not yet.* You want to know how hopeless these fucking people are? The Shia believe the secret imam is going to pop up once he sees they are fighting hard enough and creating enough fire and bloodshed in the Christian world. And the Sunnis, those geniuses, believe the same thing will happen if *they* create enough hell, except, and you won't believe this but it's true, for them it's not some ghost imam coming back, it's the fucking *Virgin Mary*! So not only do these primitive assholes think they are going to get a permanent bacchanal with completely inexperienced women in paradise if they complete their jihad by getting themselves killed, they are also helping to deliver the whole wide world into the lap of Allah Himself. Sorry, these morons have to be *managed*."

"Killed by us, you mean."

"It's worth a try!"

Ned said, "Are you through?"

Joris said, "I'm never through. And by the way we have the perfect warrior assholes to do it. The officer corps is full of *Christians* who have their own version of the end of the world. All that has to happen is the Israelis win a big battle in a place called Megiddo, something that might easily happen, it's right there on the map and there are plenty of Arabs around there. Then, of course, Jesus comes. And then what?

"I'm talking about people you can't reach by normal means, Ned. You can't make a deal. The Israelis have a doctrine. I forget what you call it, they send teams out into villages, the West Bank or wherever, and they kill the leaders showing up, and the next generation of weapons-makers, like they did with Gerald Bull who was going to build the world's largest cannon for the Iraqis and fire shells the size of Volkswagens into Israeli cities. So they sent a team to kill him. They got him in Beirut. You have to. Was that a bad idea, Ned? You won't like this, but this is what I say. *Especially with people who think getting themselves killed so they can go to paradise is a really good idea.* What I say is that a time comes when you have to kill them in large enough numbers so it interferes with their assumption that they can keep putting up mosques and proselytizing and having enough of them to look forward to covering all the patches of the earth's surface that Islamics lay claim to, Dar al-Harb, which is anywhere they're not in control of yet, look up irredentism why don't you? It's insane. And I'm saying it may be the fastest and most sparing of overall life, like Bentham, in the long run . . . it'll lead to the least overall killing, if you get it done now."

Ned could feel Joris getting happier as he pitched himself deeper into his argument. His mode had changed as he'd progressed, he was intentionally roughing up an old friend, taking a chance of alienating him. What was happening to Joris was the return from the grave of the old style of outrageous, absurdly insulting argument. One thing they had amused themselves with during the NYU years was visiting the representatives of the fossil left, all of whom had some sort of decaying perch in Manhattan, some loft, some basement. They had seen invective as an art form, and as entertainment.

Joris wouldn't stop. "Now the last thing. War is insane from the standpoint of the big democracies because it competes with fixing everything that's important, the environment, the bridges, the hundreds-of-years-old water mains. We have to stop spending on war if we're going to survive as a First World country. And you're not trying to stop some kind of all-out war that's going to solve anything. It's going to be half-assed because we don't fight wars of extermination anymore, I will say that for us . . ."

Ned broke in. "That's refreshing."

Joris said, "I'm almost through! Anyway, bankruptcy is what I was getting at. This war will do for us what losing two world wars did for the French, made them into the most diplomatic nation *on earth!*—and got them out of Africa so fast it was a blur."

Ned said, "I can't argue sitting down." He stood up. "Okay, let me rescue you, my friend. But point of order, first. You can't keep calling Muslims *Islamics.*"

"Why not?"

"It doesn't exist, that's a reason."

"It does now."

"Is Christianityics a noun? If you say it, you'll look stupid. Same with Islamics. But Islamic *is* an adjective, and so would Christianic be. Feel free to invent it." Ned was sorry he'd brought it up.

Joris said, "Okay, but before you start just realize I wasn't *advocating* anything . . ."

Ned said, "Oh but man you *are* advocating something, and I'll tell you what that is. Let me tell you the state of the world we're going to get with this Anglo-Saxon Invasion. For sure, Number One, *we will get the Shia majority taking over after we bust up Hussein's Sunni minority dictatorship.* And *then* we get the lucky Shia hooking up with their brothers in Iran . . . and big surprise putting together the second and third largest oil reserves in the world! And in the meantime the Iranians are getting the bomb so voilà presto a Shia co-prosperity sphere like the Japanese wanted in Asia . . . Okay so we the U.S. *we* go ahead and Number Two *we* use our superior technology because we haven't got enough infantry to go in and fight man to man so we use munitions we *know* will kill a lot of innocent Islamics, to use your term, and I do mean innocent because a lot of them will be people who are genuine *opponents* of the crazies, not to mention Christianics and tiny children, so in the course of winning quote unquote we end up with more Muslims hating us than ever before. Isn't that smart, Joris? We will kill lots and lots of collaterals. And Iraq can't do anything about it because they don't have the bomb, like Iran may, who knows?

"Three, anybody who hasn't got the bomb is going to go nuts getting it so they can feel safe and sound like North Korea. *Four*, whatever happened to the idea of getting bin Laden *first*, before bombing anybody? Bin Laden, who doesn't even *live* in Iraq. *Five*, you *know* it's going to turn out to be bullshit about Hussein's nuclear program, right? Lie to me and say you believe it. Say it! Six. Man you are establishing the preventive war precedent for anybody who wants to use it when they get powerful enough and mad enough. Seven, is this Seven? Anyway, I'm almost through. Seven, and I guess you can say this is still in the making, but depleted uranium is in all our weapons so the debris from all our wars from now on will go on inflicting suffering far into the future. Killing from now into the future through the bloodstreams of people who were our enemies but whose children have by a turn of the wheel become our friends. That doesn't bother you? The *future*—where our *descendants* will live? *Yours*, at least, and if I'm lucky, I'll have one or so myself."

Joris said, "Okay, so a prudentialist argument, bravo."

But now, Ned was not through. "So Eight. And this is an add-on, and I'm just about to shut up. But do you remember when Bush One egged on the southern Shia to rise up against Saddam and then let him slaughter them from the air because our no-fly zone didn't cover his helicopters? That wasn't an oversight, it was a plan . . . it reduced the power of the Shia to mess up our plan for replacing Saddam Hussein with the general of our choice.

"*Joris!* You can't be *for* the war. If we're not against this war—not even a war, an *invasion*—we're nothing. And whatever else we're for is nothing, if we don't do what we can now against this."

Ned felt an old fantasy revenge daydream show up again. The prior stars in it had been Nixon and Pol Pot and LBJ. Now it was George W. Bush. Wars end. An invisible refrigerator repository hangs over the head of the victor president. The repository is full of body parts. Anyplace the conqueror goes limbs and parts rain down on him. It would be irregular. Sometimes for a while nothing would fall. The president would begin to feel safe. But he would be wrong and the stinking bloody arms and legs and heads and feet would fall on him again. Jokes in particular would be a trigger. George Bush would never be able to tell a joke anywhere without a severed hand falling on his podium, or plate, or lap. The president stops smiling.

Ned thanked god because Joris was motioning for the pen. He felt light on his feet, as light on his feet as a two-legged marshmallow, which was a line from one of their ancient subway platform games, Absurd Similes.

Joris signed, smiling.

32 Nina was up and dressed. She was inspecting the breakfast he'd contrived for her, which was nested in cloth napkins, in a straw basket. It consisted of warm buttered toast, two hard-boiled eggs, salt and pepper shakers, an orange, a mayonnaise jar of black coffee, and silverware.

Ned said, "Gruen beat me to the yogurt but don't despair, I have a contact for you. Her name is Nadine Rose and she's very nice, and when I asked her for it and she had to deny me she said, 'I shall put it upon my list.' And those eggs were about to be deviled, but I seized them. And Nadine Rose is the person to go to for cravings. It's all arranged."

Nina sat down on the foot of the bed and began peeling one of the eggs. She said, "Thank you *so* much! This is perfect. The coffee is still warm, even! But what if I don't have any more cravings, oh my God."

Ned said, "Let's not think about that. By the way, Gruen and Joris have both signed the petition."

"That is more important to me than this *egg*! Your friends are coming through. But did you know Aristotle said, 'Oh my friends, there are no friends.' " Ned looked distressed.

Nina said, "Don't look that way. I'm sure he was just being apocryphal."

Ned was staring at her.

Nina said, "You know that was a joke, don't you? Or do you think I'm really dumb?" She thought, I know what's making him nervous, which was when we were all talking about death and I said Everybody you know's father is dead. Which no one would think was wrong if they knew *I* knew it was wrong myself, but he's nervous that they *don't* know . . . and then when I said This I'm no good at all at . . .

"No, well, I knew."

"You're so crazed on the subject of how I'm going to come across I can't stand it."

He wanted to defend himself but for the moment couldn't think of what to say.

Nina said, "There's something not on the surface between Joris and Iva. He can hardly look at her. And something happened in the hall last night that has something to do with it but I don't know what."

Ned said, "You're imagining things."

"I'm not, but nevermind. But anyway, don't worry about me. Damn it! The only reason your ectoplasmic girlfriend never embarrassed you is because she never opened her mouth, as I understand it."

"But why *ectoplasmic?*"

"Because in case you never noticed it, she looked exactly like one of those young woman forms or ghosts or whatever they were in Victorian photographs coming out of the medium's ear, flat and white. That's why. Or nostril."

"Okay," he said.

She slid out from under her breakfast and stood up and asked, "So how would you anarchists . . ."

They had a conceit, or rather Nina had a conceit he went along with because he didn't care. The conceit was that he was an anarchist pur sang, an absolutist like Bakunin, but crypto. It was all a canard based on an episode that meant nothing during the time he was running the Pacific Co-op and he had allowed a local of the Industrial Workers of the World, which still existed at that time in little nooks and crannies of the Bay Area political landscape, to distribute a recruiting appeal on the co-op premises. That was all. The treasurer of the local had vanished with the petty cash box. Nina knew the story because he'd told it to her, and he never knew when she was going to come up with some weird accusation based on it.

He said, "I know you like to keep on about my supposed anarchism, but for a change *you* go ahead and come up with a better system of your own."

"Well under anarchism would the trains run on time?"

After a pause, he said, "Trains? What trains?"

All this had only been a diversion meant to distract him so she could get into the bathroom ahead of him. She laughed as she won the race.

33 Ned was en route to the meeting-before-the-meeting, meaning a caucus of old-friends-only prior to sitting down with Iva, who was going to give them their orders on what to do or say or write for the eulogy spectacle. Elliot was descending a flight of stairs that led to the second floor, his cockpit office, and Iva's quarters. Elliot was carrying a red-rope portfolio. Ned felt some kind of strength come into him, unexpectedly, and he thought that Elliot saw it. Elliot froze on the last step above the floor.

Ned looked up at him and decided not to say I don't like your altitude and decided not to be appeasing.

Elliot looked over-groomed to Ned, as though he were on his way to a court appearance. He had a lustrous navy-blue tie on. It couldn't be, but Ned thought he saw color in Elliot's cheeks that looked like it might be some brilliant application of rouge. Ninjas with video cameras were everywhere, as usual. A TV makeup person might have done that to him.

Ned uncapped his pen. He held out the petition clipboard with the pen balanced on the petitions and in danger of falling. He tilted the clipboard. Instinctively, Elliot reached for the pen.

Ned said, "Aha, you see you have to sign this." Elliot was unhappy.

"No, I don't. I told you no, it's not necessary."

"Would you sign if I convinced you the invasion was *in fact* going to happen?"

"It's *not*."

"Make this deal with me. Give me a minute before we go in. Hear me out."

Elliot nodded. But proceeded toward the meeting room at a rapid and unfriendly pace. Ned stopped him.

Ned said, "No, not while we walk." It didn't seem unreasonable from his standpoint.

Ned said, "I *know* you'd sign if you thought the invasion *were* going to happen. And you're wrong about it, it's the plan. And forgive me, but I think your taking the position it's not going to happen isn't just laziness—I don't think that. If you don't want to appear in the list of signers that's going to take up ten pages in the *New York Times*, say so and I'll drop it. Maybe you have business reasons. But what I think is that you can't stand to think about it, and a way of nullifying a gruesome possibility is to make yourself believe it's not going to happen. I guess there's enough uncertainty about everything that that's an option. I do it myself. But this is real. The petitions go to Congress on Monday and you should sign for the same reason Pascal said you should be a Christian, because the Christians might be right about God and hell and everything so there was nothing to lose. If you stop the invasion, children who are alive and well today will keep breathing. Lots of them. The four of us have to be on the petition and you're the only one who isn't." Elliot said as he signed, "I'm not reading it."

34 It was just one more thing she had to conquer disappointment over. She was walking an oval circuit in the annoying living room. She was partial to earth tones *herself*, but *enough*. The boys were sequestered, getting their marching orders for the eulogy part of the memorial service. She had been excluded in a nice way she couldn't complain about. Somebody had dropped hints that it could get a little emotional in there, giving her the impression that she might be a hindrance to that, which had been enough. Let them, she thought. By all means let them have soft deep feelings together for a change, with no one watching, go.

Truly all she wanted was observer status. Because she liked to see Ned in action in disputes or presentations. She had missed a big argument with Joris already. She would have liked to be a spectator for that. There was a definiteness in Ned that came out beautifully sometimes, depending. It was different than the knee-jerk obduracy that everybody mistook for toughmindedness. She couldn't wait to see him stand and deliver at the memorial. She had faith. Suddenly, she had the answer to the question of why men with curly hair were treated in a certain way. It was because their hair analogically called up lambswool and lambs were lambs, not lions. She was not going to tell him.

She would wait calmly until they were through. She seated herself at the far end of the sofa next to the basket of quarterlies. She thrust her hand into the heap and pulled out one of the periodicals at random, the *Journal of the History of Childhood*, still in its wrapper. No thanks, she thought. *Disturb nothing*, she commanded herself as though the living room was a crime scene, or were one. Either way. She tried to fit the *Journal* back into the stack at roughly the place it had come from.

Outdoors it wasn't enticing. The sky was gray. She felt like doodling. Secretly she was proud of her doodles, because they weren't doodles. They were complete odd little pictures. She had the impulse to draw a figure in outline of a naked male giant with a flight of stairs running up to his anus and another flight of stairs running up to his mouth, but better not, because someone might chance by and casually ask her what she was drawing. Her doodles could be framed if anybody made frames small enough.

She was getting used to the media swarm. A ninja flashed past. One of the ninjas, a young Frenchman with long hair, a child, really, had tried to be friendly to her.

In the morning she'd said to Ned It's going to take all day to figure out what I can't wear. But it had worked out all right. There were conflicts. There were the funerary considerations. There was the need to try to blot out the image of the world's most beautiful woman not counting Iva, the tremulous Claire.

She was getting a funny idea. If it worked she would be able to flaunt mystifyingly accurate information about the secret discussions the men were having. They were meeting behind her back, literally, on the other side of the living room wall. Looking hard, she was detecting a long narrow lozenge set into the wall and two spots on it that must be hinges. It was a barely visible rectangle with an irregularity down the right side that was undoubtedly where the door could be pulled open. It was a closet, in short. The opened door would clear the end of the sofa. If she could get into it unobserved, and if it was reasonably empty and there was room for her, she could press her ear against the back of the closet and listen to some of the proceedings. She had perfect hearing. Because he was older, Ned would occasionally stop and wonder if or when they should make long-term-care plans. She hated nursing homes generically and her position was that they would only enroll when one of them became too weak to do the Heimlich maneuver. Getting into the closet would be easy enough if it wasn't locked.

She thought, Should I do this?

She knew she should wait and read. She was surrounded by reading matter in that room. A wave of resentment passed over her. She thought, I'm a constant reader . . . I signed a letter to the *Chronicle* book page as Constant Reader, when they had one . . . I read more than Ned! . . . my family culture was better than his in terms of grammar and I knew when I was still tiny that there was no such month as Febuary and no such word as nother.

Getting into the closet would be easy enough because she could start by just idly peering into it and then if the coast was clear hopping in and closing the door behind her.

God what have I done? she thought. There was no air to speak of. When she got out she was going to smell worse than her cedar-sachet-smelling insane mother. And she was about to cough. No, she was not. Yes she was, she was going to cough. The wire coat hangers she was trying to keep control of were making a racket. There was a pool of them on the floor of the closet that she hadn't noticed.

She was attempting to remain stock-still. The wall was unconscionably thick and these characters seemed to be arguing in murmurs, if they were arguing at all. This was not a good environment. She had gained *nothing* by putting herself in this predicament. The crouch she was forcing herself to assume to get her ear against the wall was painful and not working.

Someone had heard something. Someone was fiddling with the closet door.

A maid pulled it open. She thanked God she knew her name, which was Norma. The woman was astonished to see her bent over there in the darkness.

"Norma, hi. I was trying to hear what the men were talking about. You know they are being so secretive, Norma. Please don't tell on me. It would be humiliating, okay?"

"No problem," Norma said.

35 He had to find Nina to let her know about the mutiny. It had been a real mutiny and it had been great. Where was she, his Soft Gem? It was impossible to keep track of her. He filled his lungs with sun-sweetened air, which was a little poetic. It was drier out, today. Maybe Nina would lay off referring to the estate as the water park.

These days he could never locate Nina because she had invented a role for herself. She was a CPA and she was transposing her skills into investigative activities nobody had asked her to undertake. If only he could think of something for her to do other than snooping around. Clearly she thought she was going to uncover the secret gestalt behind the arrangements between Douglas and Iva, and Elliot—who appeared to Nina to have managed the family into bankruptcy, although if that was the case, why didn't he mind Nina's browsings in Douglas's stuff?

Nina saw it as a bad opera. You have a mind like a tweezers, he had said to her once, making her laugh. He had left her in the living room. Where was she now? It was warm. She'd said she wanted to look at the physic garden but she wasn't there, he could tell from where he stood. There were so many places to look for her. Her investigations came from two things. One was sheer Funktionslust. She always had to be busy. And the other was that she wanted to be his best friend. And she had criticisms of his old milieu of friends, and resentments about them. All his life he had wanted a strong and present friend. His only sibling, his older brother, had been abducted into piety, absence, the Salesian House of Studies, priesthood. They had never been friends. Nina understood it all and wanted to undo it, be his total friend, which he understood, because of course she was. And she was somewhere around there, but where?

Elliot should have seen it coming. I led the way, Ned thought. First he had led the refusal to produce short little scripts on assigned subdivisions of Douglas's life. And he had learned something in the process that was new to him. He looked forward to telling Nina about it. When Elliot had been listing some of Douglas's contributions, articles, on matters of substance, he had mentioned one, an opinion piece in the *Financial Times* about the European Monetary Union. Apparently Douglas had been skeptical of its prospects and had sarcastically described it as Jean Tinguely's Last and Greatest Creation, the joke of course being that Tinguely specialized in art object machines that destroyed themselves when they were plugged in. And surprisingly, Joris had said that he was in effect its author. The two of them had been talking and Douglas had written up Joris's thoughts, including the Tinguely conceit, and turned them into an op-ed piece supposedly by him which he sent to someone he knew at the *Financial Times*. They took it. Douglas sent Joris a copy of the issue containing it, along with a thank-you note! Joris had been cool with it, and what he was telling the group wasn't for the record.

So, it had been conceded that they could write on whatever aspect of Douglas's life they chose to. So then part two of the mutiny had been that nobody was going to grant script approval to Elliot or Iva or anybody. Elliot was going to have to trust them to solve the problem of overlapping. He'd had no choice.

Ned saw Nina. She was in conversation with someone he couldn't make out, near one of the media trailers. She waved, but continued talking to her friend. He thought, God damn her, in a way. He knew the name of the guy she was talking to but he couldn't remember what it was. Nina had talked to him several times, and he was French. Ned wanted to tell her the Joris story.

She was taking her time coming to him. He was standing on a rude bark-chip jogging path that ran close to the perimeter of the manse on three sides but looped out and away on the west side, down toward the gorge where Douglas had died. Ned guessed he would never jog. He was going to stop feeling guilty over it. There was no time in his life. Apparently he was blocking the way of three stately plump black turkeys. They were fearless. Possibly they were pets of some sort. He stepped aside for them. The story was that Douglas had once had a pet peacock. Pets would die when the fire came to Iraq. He thought, Americans love pets more than they love mankind. Maybe some agitation could be built around harm to animals. The turkeys were gross. They were unpleasant to look at and Nina was going to wonder aloud what could possibly be the evolutionary advantage of that bell-pull-like excrescence attached to the chest of the males. Survival advantages were a recurring concern of hers, and he would invent notional answers to amuse her. He could tell from Nina's expression that she had news of her own.

As he explained what had happened at the meeting with Elliot he realized that although she was nodding she was only half listening. She wanted to talk herself.

She said, "I learned some fascinating things about your friend Douglas."

"Such as?"

"Such as this. Well, he was kind of a man of mystery. He took something called *special commissions*. Which means that he did work for the German Bundes-something and for the Israelis."

"You mean verifying documents and that sort of thing?"

She was staring at the turkeys, who seemed reluctant to leave them behind. She said, "What in God's name is the use of the disgusting ropey thing that big male has on his neck? You'd think it would get tangled in the underbrush and hinder escape from predators. Maybe the lady turkeys find it attractive, maybe because it suggests macho with regard to underbrush."

Ned said, "That's definitely it. So we can move on."

She said, "Well verifying documents and maybe a lot more. Maybe helping his clients make perfect forgeries no one could detect."

"Ah this is ridiculous. Who told you this?"

"A source! And why do you think the Israeli consul general from New York is expected?"

"I have no idea. I mean I'm sure the Israelis appreciate his work on the Dreyfus *carnets*. Anyway, it's the consul from *Newark*, not New York."

"Same thing."

"No it is not."

"Anyway, he did *something* for them. And he got money in odd ways. He was paid a huge amount for writing a screenplay for a movie called *Tambov* that was never produced. It was about a remote province in Russia during the revolution where all the defectors and deserters who were sick of killing fled to and formed their own army against all the others. It was a mélange. They were communists and monarchists, anarchists like you of course, anybody who was sick of war and killing—oh and they had a green flag. Just plain green."

"So are you saying it was laundered money? Wait, I think I know who told you all this."

He squinted back in the direction she'd come from to see if the culprit, the guy she had been talking to, was still there. He was. And Ned should have realized it earlier. His name was Jacques and he was wearing a signature matelot jersey, echt French.

"Oh God, you've been talking to that French guy, Jacques, I forget his last name."

"I'm getting forgetful too. And oh, remind me to remember to tell Ma about my food adventures around here. When she figured out I was eating stuff I've never eaten in my life before, like, lobster roe, she said I had to remember everything and tell her . . ."

"Don't you think I have enough on my mind? Get a memo book like I have. I don't feel like writing down entries for your gourmet life list . . ."

"Lobster roe, and sticky toffee pudding and what was the other thing—mushroom strudel, and oh, flavored salt."

"If the French guy comes over here I'm going to have to beat you."

"You're saying that like you hate the French or things French or something."

"I am God damn *not*. Actually I've talked to the guy already. He snagged me after breakfast twice. And he's okay."

"And he's jolly, Ned! At least compared to your friends. And he's against the war, sorry, the invasion. And by the way he's a squatter."

"I'm not surprised. You mean he's living in a squat commune in Lyon or someplace?"

"No no no. He's squatting *here*. He isn't official. He's a stowaway here. He's sleeping in one of the basements in the tower. And he's against the war."

Ned was annoyed. She was romanticizing her Frenchman, thinking *Jacques* was the real article, unlike *some* people she could name.

"I know he's against the war. I had to tell him twice he couldn't sign my petition because he wasn't a U.S. citizen. Politically he's fucking way off the left edge of the map. He works for an alternative FM station in Lyon called Diffusion Ravachol. He's been searching for me to give me a book by his hero Thierry Meyssan that's going to prove to me that the Pentagon was hit by a missile, not a plane . . ."

"But he's on our side at least! I wouldn't go so far as to call him a *brother* but . . ."

Ned said, "I am grinding my teeth, you may notice. It's my own fault. I made the mistake of starting off with him in my New Chardenal French. So now he thinks I speak French when in fact I hardly know what I'm saying. Oh Christ descend! He's coming to join us."

"Salut!" Jacques shouted, arriving. He was a short, eager, muscular man probably in his late thirties although he might be younger and suffering the effects of a dissipated existence. That was just a guess. His face was pear shaped, heavy around the mouth. He had his graying blond hair in a ponytail. One wing of his very full gray moustache was stained amber. He chain-smoked Gitanes, was smoking one now, and in a moment Nina and Ned would both get the chance to appreciate the considerate way he had of carrying on conversations with declared nonsmokers like themselves: he would blow plumes of smoke out laterally from the corner of his mouth. It was something to see! And Ned wondered if Nina had already noticed that. He had the trait of lowering his voice and instantaneously looking left/right before conveying bits of information he thought were important, which so far, in Ned's experience, they hadn't seemed to be. Women would like his bright blue eyes, no doubt. Jacques was a Breton, if Ned had understood him in an earlier conversation.

Jacques embraced them, Nina first and more thoroughly.

Ned had an existential problem with the Frenchman he wanted to get across. It wasn't that he didn't like him. But there was an issue.

He patted Jacques's shoulder. He turned to Nina and said, "Hey, can you help me? You took French. I want to explain something to this man. Don't make a face, just do your best. And I know he claims he speaks English but give me a break. Now listen, here's what I want to explain." Ned kept a reassuring smile on his face and again patted Jacques on the shoulder.

"Okay," Jacques said irrelevantly.

Ned said to Nina, "I want to explain up front that we differ on something. It's important. His mindset is all over the antiwar movement. Here's the thing. I see a shitty outcome of causative events I can mostly only guess at. I say we have to stop the outcome. Like the invasion. But au contraire he wants to root around in the causes, the *conspirations*, as they usually turn out to be in his opinion . . . the causes. I want to get across to him the concept of *fait accompli* if I can. We need to *forget the conspiracies*. Let history sort it out! . . . but stop the invasion." Jacques had just said what sounded like "jolie" under his breath and he had winked at Nina. Ned said very softly, to Nina, "He just winked at you."

"Oh do I know it. I'm going to France, mon ami. But you have to stop this, you're acting like we're talking in front of a horse. But I will say this, apparently they have tons of petite women stars over there. French movie stars I look like that I never heard of. He's so *acute*."

"I em a *cute*?" Jacques said.

Seize power, Ned said to himself. "Jacques, listen to me. Okay, first, comment ça va tu?" He couldn't help but notice Nina groaning loudly enough for Jacques to hear. He was going to proceed anyway and she could fuck herself.

"Bien. Bien." Jacques had had to repeat himself because he had spoken crookedly, having had the need to stick his tongue out and pick a few wayward flecks of tobacco off it. His tongue furrow was black.

Ned said, "Secondaire, il y a deux visions entre nous au contraire. A la regard de les deux . . . towers—les neuf onze *tours* . . ."

Nina whispered, subtly, she obviously thought, "Jumeau. Twin is jumeau."

"Would you please shut up," Ned replied.

Jacques said, "I understand well."

Ned, with effort, resumed. "C'est un fait accompli. Les auteurs originals, avec l'argent, peut-être, sont inconnus. Les Saudis peut-être. C'est n'importe. Et maintenant puisque les explosions de les jumeaux, nous avons un invasion, la guerre!" Ned stopped. It was too hard, although he could easily understand what Jacques was saying in French which at the moment appeared to be an invitation to them to come and visit him on the Rhône. And here Jacques swung into English. Apparently from his porch one could see "La Rhône right affront of you."

Ned thought, To be fair, it's hard to know what's a fait accompli and what isn't. He had to keep that in mind. What he wanted to say wasn't that complex. It was that there could be a conspiracy at the root of a great evil, and there could be appendages to the conspiracy, and the problem was that the outcome was the same whether there had been a conspiracy, or not. Douglas's term for the right attitude to take toward politics had been selective fatalism. The term had come up in discussions of the Kennedy assassination, which was a perfect example of a fait accompli. There was only so much social energy available for addressing evil, which never stands still. You had to forget conspiracies tout court, if that was right, and get on with the outcomes.

And then like a bird from God, Nina put it all into perfect concise French and did it too fast for him to follow. And Jacques nodded sharply and she nodded sharply and Ned felt stupid and blessed.

Ned accepted the Meyssan book. Jacques had someplace to go.

Nina said, "I don't know where it came from. It just all came back to me in a sort of flash."

Ned said, "I seem to know very little of what is going on these days. And why did he say, 'Liberté, Égalité, Maternité' when he left?"

"Because I told him I was pregnant and couldn't have sex with him."

"He asked you that?"

"Of course. He's an anarchist, like you. He asks everybody."

"I'm glad you said no."

"Good," Nina said. Then added, "I better be pregnant."

Don't ever leave me, Ned thought.

36 They were all convened, again, in the conversation-pit room. It wasn't clear why. The mutiny had taken place and it had been successful and it was supposed to be free-form when it came to the tributes they were going to give. But now it felt like Elliot wanted to take it back. Elliot was entering the room back first, attempting to close the door on some insistent person he was being emphatic with. It was Iva. He leaned against the door and he got it closed. He locked it behind his back.

Iva seemed to have departed. Ned was seated on the leather sectional at the end closest to the left-hand door. Joris was next to him but Gruen was still standing up in an apparent trance. Ned had felt faintly embarrassed when Nina said to Gruen, Did you get that cold you were getting? He reminded himself that people all up and down the cultural ladder said dumb things, like the young woman who had come to him about a homeless panhandler wandering around inside the co-op, saying of herself that when she'd seen him she'd become visibly moved, or like the *Oakland Tribune* intern who had introduced herself by saying, I'm a young journalist.

Gruen, one ear plugged with cotton, his inhaler momentarily abandoned in his right nostril, was studying what was for Elliot a strange new gait—Elliot was moving slowly and appeared to be placing his feet carefully as he proceeded, rather than ambling in the standard automatic mode. Joris tugged on Gruen's pant leg and Gruen sat down. Joris sighed, because lively knocking at the door had resumed. Tediously

Elliot retraced his steps and minimally opened the door. Iva thrust an aggrieved sliver of herself into the room. It appeared that she was wearing a Day-Glo blue velour track-suit. Nina on the other hand had been excruciating herself to dress appropriately for the different tones and phases of the moment they were caught in. A hissed exchange between Iva and Elliot ended and Iva withdrew, still angry. No doubt she wanted to be included. So did Nina, but she wasn't beating her fists on doors. What was going on would make a good libretto. Elliot began his modern-dance-like return to his station, a cubical black club chair set closely opposite the sectional. The coffee table had been dematerialized. Elliot was dressed in a well-cut high-end dark business suit. His slab-like shirt cuffs were held together by ornate cuff links featuring a gem that might well be tanzanite. In his right hand Elliot was clutching a couple of sheets of yellow legal-pad paper that had been tortured into the shape of a carrot or cypress.

Ned felt a pulse of alarm. Just for an instant, Elliot's eyes seemed magnified. Was he sick? Circumstances had conspired to make Elliot the majordomo of everything that was going on. Ned wondered how unfair he had been to Elliot. He'd really done nothing to separate the man, Elliot, from the whatever they should be called, the odious duties he'd been called on to perform. And Elliot had been just as much his friend as any of them, in the old days. With relief, Ned realized that the alarming moment had only been tears pending, but not yet sliding free, as they were doing now. Elliot was holding himself stiffly. Unexpectedly, he raised his paper creation and flicked his tears off his cheeks as they got there. It would stop. Here we are, we need to do more for Elliot, Ned thought. Ned looked into himself and concluded that he was using Elliot's long-term intermittent trouble with his back as a cover for not asking why he was walking so peculiarly.

Ned said, "El, are you okay? Is it your back?"

Elliot said, "It is, and I'll be okay. I was doing too much lifting, is all. But now I've got plenty of help and I have meds." He took tissues from a pocket and blew his nose.

Ned had an explanation for what was happening to them. It was that they had been recalled, after outbursts from Iva, which were continuing, to get them to take back their mutiny and do what they had been instructed to. They were scheduled for a tale of woe. Elliot was going to build a platform of personal stress to stand on and appeal to them from. I forgive you, Ned thought.

Elliot began. It was not a supremely well-organized pre-sentation they were getting. He had never seen a Windsor knot as monumental as Elliot's. The emphasis was on the physical, the medical, all of which was depressing and a lot of it new to him. His own life had been lived on the West Coast, away from the scene. He was feeling bad.

As the friends all knew, a couple of years after Elliot married her, Muriel had been diagnosed with ALS. Her decline was rapid. It nearly killed Elliot. Five years after they were married, the poor woman was dead. They had had only a brief period of normal married life. Muriel had declined rapidly: to a walker, to a wheelchair, to bedridden, to a nursing home. She was an only child, and had expected to be an heiress, but her father had died leaving behind a substantial burden of debt. That had been a surprise.

Something confessional was coming.

Elliot was a stockbroker. Under the pressures he was describing he had been pulled toward more and more risk in the deals he was making, which had worked out bigtime initially, he was saying, with a stress on *initially*. "Emphasis on initially," Joris muttered, and then he said something Ned didn't understand. He repeated it for Ned. "Qualcomm."

Ned knew what Qualcomm was. It was a stock that had soared and then crashed. He hadn't known that it was a major holding of Douglas's and Iva's. Joris knew a lot. If fascism ever came he would pick Joris to be in the maquis with, and, okay, Gruen if he lost weight. Ned wondered if Joris had been put into Qualcomm by Elliot, too, and Gruen.

At forty-five, Elliot had undergone a prostatectomy. This was new. Apparently it was new to all of them. There was a group murmur of sympathy. Ned felt something in his genitals, not his physical genitals but in the idea of his genitals.

There was a bevy of details on the protracted healing process. One detail that was tough to hear was Elliot's account of discovering, through an embarrassing incident, that he had become insensitive to a faint odor of urine it seemed he was carrying around with him although he was faithful about changing his pads. Changing them timeously, Douglas would have said, during the phase when he was pointlessly trying to lard Briticisms into everyday discourse at NYU. Arvacado. They all wanted to hear the grim minutiae of Elliot's path back to continence. Or rather, they didn't and they did. It could all go under the heading of cautionary information because every man in the room was entering the prostate trouble zone. And of course crouching there was the *other* thing.

The other thing was impotence. Of course impotence would probably be the universal masculine fate if you lived long enough. But everything is timing, Ned thought. On the plane he'd read in something that the human body stops aging at ninety. So . . . something to look forward to. Elliot had the traditional open prostatectomy. Now there was the robotic option. Ned had read about it. Elliot had suffered postoperatively. He was not giving them the *Reader's Digest* version of his tribulations, either.

Elliot said, "What you realize is that it takes away something you were used to and depended on." It was difficult for him, where he was going with this. Ned was full of sympathy. Elliot was grimacing. The friends waited.

Elliot was saying, "You lose the stupid imaginary availability of the women you run into. I was a widower when this struck, and I had been for a while, so I was single, you could say. Also the example of getting my continence back in less than a year turned out to be misleading. But this thing about women, until it's gone, you never realize how calming, automatically calming, it is, to have these fantasy images running in your head, this imagery. And then the material basis of the imagery is gone and of course you have the history of getting lucky in the past in the fairly recent past that supported the imagery."

They were all uncomfortable. Ned wanted urgently to think about something else, something amusing if possible, and felt cowardly. Nina would find Elliot's existential discoveries, or discovery, interesting. But he knew if he told her she would say, So how well does that describe *your* inner life, by the way?

His mind wasn't wandering, it was resisting. He didn't want to think about death or impotence, either one. Since Nina, he had been living in almost a burlesque show with sex and comedy going on nonstop after the years when it had been so otherwise. Take blubalub, for example, he thought. Blubalub was a conceit of Nina's. One summer they had stayed for a month in a cottage near Stinson Beach. And the cottage's Dutch door had opened directly on the driveway. So once when he was coming back from the mailbox she had opened the top section of the Dutch door and stood there topless and invited him to put his face between her breasts and nuzzle side to side, which she'd referred to as blubalub. Trees kept anyone in the vicinity from seeing. So then she'd said blubalub was something for the UPS driver, something she had worked out with him one day when Ned was off swimming, and that when Ned had come to the door just then and she was topless, it had been a mistake because she'd been expecting the UPS guy, with whom the deal was that he would come to the Dutch door and she would let him have blubalub and he would give her the parcel meant for them and then she would get to go out to the truck and take her pick of any other parcel she wanted. Ned wanted it all to go on forever. On his very tall tombstone he wanted inscribed at the top Fun Had, and all the rest would be a list of things dating from Nina coming into his life. He knew he had to keep it to himself.

He got back to Elliot, who apparently was doing pretty well with erections. He was saying that getting used to orgasms that produced only a puff of air had taken some doing. Ned was a little unprepared for the degree of intimacy Elliot was providing. Their life together on Second Avenue must have been more decorous than he remembered.

Now this is interesting, Ned thought. Elliot was implying or imparting something that seemed cryptic. It was about a woman who had been his lover. He was being flowery. He was being obscure and intricate in his references to whoever she was. Nobody knew what to say.

Ned got up, feeling he had to. He said, "What a thing for you, man." He wondered if others would want to say something, too, but Elliot was moving rapidly on. The pitch was coming. Ned sat down again.

Elliot was retracing the part of the story that had to do with Douglas's economic situation. It was a crisis. There was nothing else to call it. A lot of his investments for the family had been under-hedged, as he put it, and Douglas had plowed much more into the physical estate than he should have. He was profligate. And Douglas had done that on his own, not letting anyone grasp the dimensions of it. Even Iva had been left out of Douglas's finances. This place they were in was surrounded by collapsing walls of debt, was the way Elliot expressed it. And here was the Elliot who had been a star in the Drama Club at NYU, always in character parts because of his unusual height. Emoting, was what he was doing.

Elliot wanted it to be about friendship. Their friend Douglas was an important figure in European political culture, because of the Dreyfus *carnets*, and the Kundera journal, and a string of other less-well-known interventions, he wasn't exactly sure what they should be called, Elliot said. A documentary on Douglas for Eurovision that was being made now, here, all around them, was going to be essential to saving the day for Iva and Hume. Two German foundations and two Israeli foundations were *this close* to setting up a research center on forgery as propaganda, right there, funding it and setting Iva up to superintend and represent it, which he thought they would have to agree she was superbly qualified to do. Douglas had been in discussion with them for over a year. Elliot paused.

Ned had been correct. The pitch was on. Elliot was saying that he had to be frank. And what he meant by that was that Douglas had not always been polite or politic in his dealings with people in his realm of contacts, in his performances at colloquia and so on, in Europe. He had made some enemies. And there were certain names that had been expected to come over for this event who weren't going to. Douglas had made enemies on the far right in Europe and as they all knew things were shifting and the right was coming back in spots here and there in Europe. So the picture was changing.

Ned willed Elliot to get it over with. He knew what was happening, but he resented having to concentrate to see the inner mechanism exposed. Elliot was blunt about what he wanted. They were supposed to humanize Douglas. Elliot even used the word. Joris said sotto voce, "He means *sell* him," just before Elliot said, "It's our job to sell Douglas for Iva and Hume."

Elliot wanted to go back to the plan as it had originally been. He wanted the friends to divide up Douglas's life in a particular way. He wanted them to rescind their prior refusal. He gave his ideal division of labor to them quickly, and with a certain amount of shame showing. Joris would do something on Douglas as an outdoorsman, referencing all the camping and long-distance hiking and the Appalachian Trail forays of their student days. Joris looked absolutely astonished but said nothing. Elliot would supply Joris with some other information relevant to that, environmental groups Douglas had supported, or been affiliated with, and so on.

Ned was sorry for Joris. He wondered what in hell he himself was going to be asked to take up. If they'd devoted time to camping on six weekends over four years that would be a lot, unless Elliot was counting climbing up onto some of the larger rocks in Central Park and sitting there reading in the sun for a while. They'd joined the Outing Club and quit after one semester. The club had included non-student participants from the school's neighborhood and they had found themselves in a hiking party led by a vigorous old woman who, pointing eastward from the top of Storm King at a line of smoke rising from some valley, had informed them that that was the location of hell.

Elliot had managed this pretty cleverly, and Ned felt disarmed, and Elliot had, after all, signed his petition.

Gruen's assignment was to give a brief appreciation of Douglas as a friend. And then Elliot said that he wanted a few of Douglas's pranks mentioned, which he would consult with Gruen on, as to which ones, exactly. Ned couldn't look at Gruen and was now busy feeling dumbfounded at his own assignment. He was expected to give a short paper on Douglas's *philosophy*, call it, and Elliot *had a paper already prepared for Ned to read or refer to.* In fact, Elliot had drafts and notes for everyone. They were going to keep things crisp. It would be a panel. Elliot would go into the highlights of Douglas's career, the great cases.

"All for one," Ned heard Gruen say.

Elliot took three number-ten envelopes containing their scripts from an inside pocket and handed them out.

It was interesting to Ned that he, Joris, and Gruen understood without exchanging a word that they were all going to participate in this travesty.

The meeting was over. Ned led the way and opened the door, to find Iva standing close, directly in the way, a pained, anxious smile on her face. She was waiting for a sign from Elliot and she must have gotten it because her face relaxed.

37 Nina was telling herself that she was pregnant more or less constantly, but sometimes she slipped and it came out audibly and it was beginning to annoy Ned. She was hungry. There was to be no more fine dining. She'd been told by her friend Nadine Rose that meals were going to be mess hall style now and Nadine had also told her that Iva and Elliot would be eating privately. If, in their frenzy, they were eating at all, Nina thought.

Ned was in a bleak mood. Apparently the group's decision to mutiny had been overturned and he didn't want to go into it and now he had to write something about Douglas's philosophy. And Ned was saying, mostly to himself, things like *What* philosophy? *Antifascism*?

All this brooding around wasn't good. She said, "You think the self is something like a hardboiled egg. That's your image of it. But it isn't, it's something like a deck of cards."

He ignored her.

They had made their way to one of the manse's highest decks and Ned was at work, stretched out on a patio lounger, talking brusquely into his microrecorder. He was getting agitated, she could tell. Because he was occasionally making a fist. He wanted her to be quiet and read something until he was through. Earlier he had said to her My darling you're going to have to talk to yourself for a while. He'd removed his shoes and socks and was hanging his feet out into space, his ankles supported by a crossbar of the railing. His feet looked like small wings. And they would look more like wings if he would stop wriggling his toes like a mental patient.

Ned said, "Don't talk to me."

"I'd love to."

Really she wanted to provoke his attention. It wasn't fair, because he was struggling to write something he didn't want to. But maybe a break would help him. She would try to get his attention only once. She had plenty of ammunition. She could tell him about Jacques offering her a joint but wouldn't.

She said, "I wish I could get my karma overwith in a week or ten days instead of my whole life."

Ned frowned at her.

"Okay then," she said.

She was starving. Ned had perfect feet, more like drawings of feet. She had a hilarious little toe, as in hideous. Two things were annoying at present. She knew she was going to make a pest of herself at the buffet because Nadine Rose had told her that franks and beans were going to be one of the main dishes and she was going to ask if they were the nitrite kind of franks. She wouldn't eat those, on behalf of her baby. The other thing that was bothering her was that she had something substantial to offer to Ned that might be useful for his discussion of Douglas's philosophy, so called, absorbed on her own in something. But she was born to comment. And he had no idea where she'd gone. He had checked their room and the bathroom they shared with Joris and Gruen. There had been an alien odor in the bathroom. Nina had said something about letting Jacques use their shower to freshen up. So, obviously that had happened. He had no defensible reason for objecting to it.

And if he did say anything, he knew what would come next. It would be the next big fun canard. She was going to say that not only was he Mikhail Bakunin but he was a Francophobe. And he wasn't. For example, he thought the French had the best *names* in the world like Loik le Floch Prigeant and Fustel de Coulanges and Choderlos de Laclos.

Fuck me, he thought. The day was bright and mild. The madding crowd of service and media people was still growing. When would it stop? He made out Gruen down the slope toward the gorge talking into his cell phone. Gruen is good and I'm a shit, he thought. Because Gruen called his mother all the time. Ned called nobody except associates, which was all he had, really. And unless he wanted to yank his brother away from his duties giving absolutions and praying nonstop or whatever he spent his time doing, he had no family to speak of, nobody to call about personal things. It was melancholy but it was true. His father had died fast, of cancer, at sixty, just after retiring. He remembered his father signalizing his retirement by unstrapping his wristwatch and declaring that he was never going to wear it again. His father had been the office manager of a company in El Cerrito that made bedsprings. Amazingly, as he'd learned very late in their relationship, his father had gone into factory work as an evangelist for the Trotskyist group he had covertly belonged to for a couple of years in his youth. He'd been elevated from the shop floor to management because he had a knack for it. His main piece of fatherly advice to Ned had been Stick with the Jews, meaning to emulate Jewish rationality and book worship. His mother and father had become more and more alienated from one another as his mother's embrace of ultra Catholicism had tightened. Not long after his father's death, when his mother was only fifty-five, she'd been killed in Fruitvale, in a crosswalk, by a drunk driver. His share of the settlement had paid for his tuition at NYU, a place his father had liked the idea of, for him. He didn't know why but as far back as he could remember his brother had never been friendly to him. Whether it was a question of temperaments or was somehow connected to the fact that their mother had so obsessively been grooming her firstborn for the Church, he didn't know. His first dried apricot had been given to him by his brother with the information that it was a human ear. His brother had been close only to their mother.

Ned decided to follow Gruen at a distance. Joris had told him that Gruen would go occasionally to stand meditatively by the gorge, alone, every day.

Gruen stopped at a high point upstream from the death site. He stood there. Ned halted. It was solemn. He liked Gruen for this. And then, startlingly, Gruen reared back and spat as hard as he could into the air above the stream. It was a jarring thing. Ned walked halfway to Gruen and shouted at him, "What was *that*?"

Gruen turned and was awkward for a moment. Ned joined him. Gruen said, "I was seeing if I could spit across."

"Thank God," Ned said.

Gruen said, "I've been wondering about it. The answer is I can't." Ned thought, Casually spitting in public used to be a male prerogative, sort of . . . it could go on Douglas's list of deprivations that men were experiencing. A campaign against spitting in the street had been conducted in his junior high, and he remembered one of the campaign posters: If You Expectorate Don't Expect To Rate.

Gruen was looking much healthier. On impulse, Ned embraced him. "Have you seen Nina?" Ned asked him.

"I have," Gruen said, and patted himself on the back of his neck. Ned was not understanding Gruen's gesture. "Do you know she trimmed me up?" Gruen asked.

Will she never cease? Ned thought.

What had happened was that Gruen had found her in an amiable conversation with Hume touching on the problem with his ankle, which was improving, and his hairstyle, which she said she loved but that could stand improvement. So they had all gone together to the house and secured barbering tools and she had been good enough to give each of them a trim. Gruen said, "Man, she *razed* those humps off his head and I got scared but he seemed to like the results."

Ned asked, "Do you know where she is now?"

"I don't, but she's having a rendezvous with that French guy someplace, who *by the way* tied up the bathroom for half an hour. She's very busy. She's got a bunch of papers she wants to show you. Where she went to find the French guy, I don't know."

"Thank you, my friend," Ned said.

He found her in the physic garden. Her back was to him. He beheld her for a couple of minutes. The sentence *I stand here lonely as a turnstile* came to him and was unwelcome and he shook it away. It was the pickup line Douglas had used to get Claire's attention in the Figaro, in the dim past. Nina was standing on the curb of the uninhabited fish pond, slumped, dejected seeming. "Don't jump," he said.

When he and Nina had parted earlier, she'd said You're being fairly abominable. And then she'd said, Oh you're all so busy playing into one another's hands. She'd been irritated, but not seriously. She was glad to see him. She was carrying a clutch of papers.

"I gave Hume a haircut," she said. "Wait till you see him. It's *much* better."

There was a park bench available. He stamped down the weedy overgrowth surrounding it and tested the seat for dryness. Nina looked tired. She sat down, relieved. He sat next to her.

"I'm liking him," she said.

Ned said, "I can see that. Joris has been telling me more about him. Even when he gets into trouble there's something original about it, it sounds like to me, although original is probably the wrong word. I don't mean to excuse anything. When Hume was being harassed by an older girl at school he decided to follow her around saying *I moan, Naomi.* And when the principal yelled at him to leave Naomi alone Hume shouted back *Rail, liar!* and defended himself by saying he'd just been practicing creating palindromes. The principal had kind of liked Hume before and had said it was clever when the boy introduced the word tomorning into classroom discourse, Hume's point being that it was exactly like tonight and today, so it stood to reason it was a real word. Now, what have you got there?"

She selected a sheet of paper from her collection and

handed it to Ned, saying, "This was bookmarking a section in the *Study Guide to DSM-IV*, the part on Borderline Personality Disorder. These other papers were in the book too."

He began reading and he grimaced and she said, "I know."

What he was looking at was a photocopy of a second-grade English composition of Hume's. The text was crudely typed. On a letterhead cover sheet, the principal of Tremper Consolidated had written, in a forceful hand:

Please look over the herewith:
The names of the lunchroom staff
are not fictitious. One name has been
misspelled, where Hume has written
"Venerable" for "Venable." I have of
course passed it to the nurse, but I am
eager to have your comments or those
of any colleagues at Mental Health you
think might shed light. I sent
you material on this pupil last year
and you were most helpful. One
other thing I should mention is
that it has been reported to me
that Hume was organizing a raffle
whose 25 cent ticket would allow
the winner to go behind a bush with
one of the female pupils in order to
watch her urinate, but there were
denials by the girl, so no evidence.
Looking to hear,
Jack Ryder

Principal
Tremper Consolidated

Hume's composition was entitled THE GREATEST
OF ALL LUNCHTIMES AT TREMPER SCHOOL.

Oh my a hord gathered! Dork
girls screamed. Ken the mastermind
of the cretens cried out something
or other. There are mostly boy cretens
but a few girls are too. More hords
came, like lackeys and vermin. Mrs.
Venerable opened the doors. She
has one shrinked arm and one regular
arm.

Another hord came in from soccer
practicing. They were mostly varlets
with some poltroons and lackwits
strewed in. The head cook Mrs.
Murdock stated "Our vegetable
today is lovely fresh skunk cabbage."
So the atheletes began cheering,
because they loved the breakfast
of scrambled snake eggs of that
very morn. "Oh please don't forget
the stink weed salad, if you please,"
said Mrs. Murdock, who also had a
job as a murderer and stabbed peoples
eyes out with frozen carrots and killed
peoples pets by feeding them left overs

she sneaked into other peoples houses
with.

Ned said, "I'm working on my assignment, you know,
but what is *my* philosophy, Nina? My philosophy is No Hitting. I don't have time for a philosophy."
   "Ned please don't tear yourself up. You're a *fine* person!
You keep forgetting that. Do you want to know something I
told Ma when I first met you, when we first started dating?
I said, Even his id is nice."
   "Well, that's pretty beside the point. Anyway, thinking about Douglas's philosophy is a laugh. At one point
we were all supposed to hate Immanuel Kant because he
singlehandedly sold out the Enlightenment. I remember
the whole thing. He authorizes religion to be in charge of
any question where certainty is impossible. *Religion within
the Limits of Reason Alone* 1793. Do you know what stro-
mata means? It's Greek for rag rug, and that's what *Douglas*
called his philosophy."
   "You're overreacting to this task for some reason."
   "Okay. Now I'm not." He resumed reading.

The cooks have a trick langwich.
They can talk like humans but they
can also talk to each other by their
behinds.

WE ARE TALL! the atheletes said.
"Some of you are" the girls screamed.

Nina said, "That's only the first page."
Ned said, "That's enough. But does it get worse? Don't

tell me if it does. I blame a lot of this on Douglas. It took him a long time to take fatherhood seriously, I think. When we were in school he said if he had children and one was a daughter he was going to name her Groucha or Tendril. And a boy was going to be Dagwood. He was presumably kidding. And how hard would it be for Hume to pick up that Douglas loved him to be outrageous? I know I told you about the time Hume invented his own personal practical joke, the one where he dipped all the points of the sharpened pencils on Douglas's desk in Elmer's Glue. Douglas put it in a fax, he was so proud of it."

Nina said, "Your friend had a compulsion."

"You don't see me arguing with you. There were the gallstones. A retired surgeon was a friend of the family and they were visiting him in Kingston. Douglas notices a jar of gallstones in the living room. The old surgeon had been accumulating them for years. The short of it is that Douglas begs the guy to give them to Hume as scientific curios. What Douglas actually had in mind was for Hume to use them in the battlements of the forts he built for his toy soldier armies, which he did."

"Grotesque," Nina said.

Ned said, "And Douglas would never give it a rest. The four of us would go out walking in the Village on the way to a show or opening and fucking Douglas would jump inside a restaurant we were passing and shout in a giant voice *Save room for pie.*"

"Gruen has pranks. Remind him about that."

"Good idea. And go ahead and show me anything else you think I can take. I can take anything."

. . .

Nina considered her papers. She said, "I have something from fourth grade. He was in the Steiner school then. I want to read it to you. You're going to like him better."

"I don't dislike him. I just said I felt sorry for him. And I blame Douglas, anyway. It's a rant. He was a second grader dealing with rage, letting it out, and it's not so terrible anyway. And who knows, maybe that's better than trying to digest a doorknob for twenty years. Read me something, go."

The Thanksgiving Meaning

Twas one of the first Thanksgivings;
But none of the best, we know,
For this Thanksgiving, I'm sorry to say
was full of sleet and snow.

But this doesn't mean that Thanksgiving's bad;
Or that it has no meaning.
Thanksgiving's a wonderful thing;
For it is a time of feasting and dancing;
What a wonderful time to sing!

The Pilgrims came from faraway England
In a little ship called the Mayflower;
They came to America freedom to find,
And could worship every hour!

Not only could they worship for long,
But worship as they pleased,
But good and great as Thanksgiving is,

The Pilgrims were not quite eased;
For by the end of the very first winter,
Half of them were deceased.

They sat in silence. "There's just one more," she said. "It's not by Hume."

"What is it?" Ned asked.

"It's a poem by Douglas, I mean the beginning of one, and it's pretty recent. You'll be sad." She handed it to him.

The poem fragment was in Douglas's familiar spineless loose cursive hand.

My son Hume had two friends
when he was very young

Belgerman and Johnsont
Invisible but always on his
side

Now he's lost
Please go and find him,

39 She liked Ned in jeans. The two of them were a symphony in denim but it didn't matter. It was appropriate for what they were doing. They were bushwhacking. She stopped to study the beautifully sketched little map Hume had given her. She had also seen some other artwork by Hume that was lying around in Douglas's studio, or office, but she wasn't going to share it with Ned, necessarily. One had been a large cartoon head of a woman who looked something like Iva, wearing earrings that were little globular cages with tiny men trapped in them.

"Ned, stop brooding."

"Let's get this hike over with," he said.

Hume had provided her with a route map to a place he wanted her to see, on, as he'd put it, his side of the mountain. That apparently included the entire reach of forest on the other side of the death stream, all the way up to the next ridge. The ascent to Hume's Inspiration Point wasn't exactly a gratuitous thing. It was more an act of solidarity with the boy. The spot meant something to Hume. She wondered if Hume might come to visit them in the future. It was just an idea.

Ned was scowling into his notebook.

Nina said, "We can stop for a while if you want. Or do you have something you want to say to me?"

"Yes, I want to say something, but what? I'm feeling bad. I called Don at Christmas, but I should do it more. I have a brother who has to get permission to come to the phone. But I'm going to do it more often anyway."

She wondered why he was bringing up Don. Ned was estranged from his brother and he didn't like to talk about it. And her past efforts to get him to be friendlier toward Don had been met with a confused resistance. It was complicated. Her impression from meeting him had been that Don was gay. She'd made the mistake of asking Ned if he assumed he was. The timing was bad, because this had been during one of the surges in the Church's pedophile scandals when Ned was stomping around referring to the Roman Catholic Church as a criminal enterprise. Ned had been

impatient with her. He didn't care. What he cared about
was that he didn't have a brother.

"It was good you called Don, but that was months and
months ago. And these men . . . I don't think you should be
complaining about friendship. These are decent, intelligent
men, and they're interesting. And say something substantive to Gruen! Ask him what he's reading! Half the time he
has a folded-up copy of the *New York Review of Books* in
his pocket . . ."

Ned said, "I agree with everything you say." They
resumed their climb.

Their destination had been this overlook, a small clearing
open at one end on a fine northwest view of rows of medium
hills. A semicircle of hemlocks closed the venue at the back
and on the sides. Getting there had taken them through
raw brush, tangled deadfall, and, here and there, around
stinking sumps. The rough little meadow felt untouched. If
you got too close to the view, you could step off into a sheer
drop. It was a lover's leap. They stood for a while watching
the grassy field around them creasing in the warm wind.

Ned said, "Somebody appreciated this spot in the past.
There's an overturned sundial back in the brush, and I'll bet
it was set up here originally." He was looking melancholy.

He found a tree to lean against. He brought out his
notebook and began to write in it. And when Nina drifted
toward him with the intent of being granted a look at what
he was writing, he bridled. She was used to it. He had said,
"My notebook is my unconscious." And now he was going to
say that he often wrote down things that he couldn't under-

stand later. We don't hear ourselves, she thought. Ned said, "Sometimes I can't even read what I've written." She couldn't help being curious about what he was writing, but based on his asides on the trip up through the woods her guess was that he had turned his attention to thinking of subject matter for Gruen. She knew him. His own assignment, he hated.

"Why did Hume want us to come up here?" Ned asked.

"He didn't say but I know he thought we'd like it."

"I wonder if Douglas ever came up here."

She was sick of everything linking back to Douglas. She was starting to feel like Douglas was Rebecca, ready to come to life and jump down out of a picture frame over the fireplace.

Ned was still writing. She would leave him alone. She walked around moodily enjoying the ambiance as well as she could.

"What is it?" he asked.

"Nothing. Oh, well. Do you think you were homophobic in the old days?" She genuinely had no idea why she was asking that question.

Ned was startled. He closed his notebook. He said, "You're kind of uncanny, asking me that right now. Because what I've been doing is recalling and rejecting stuff, prank-related stuff Gruen might use. We made up gay comic strips. I remember Prince Variant . . . and Vaseline Alley, and Gene Autre. There was no animus behind it, I don't think. I don't remember, if there was."

Ned was thinking hard, she could tell. She wasn't liking herself right then. She regretted the question she'd asked.

Ned said, "I mentioned Dale, a gay black guy who was part of the group . . . he wasn't out of the closet, exactly, but we all knew, and it was irrelevant. He was just part of the group. Sophomore year he transferred to McGill. Wouldn't you like to have a cabin built right here?"

"*No.* And don't change the subject."

"I wasn't. We've talked about this before. You think my brother is gay. You know, Stonewall had happened around the corner just a couple of years before we got to NYU. We weren't troglodytes."

"Was Dale around for Prince Variant et al.?"

"There wasn't anything to be around *for*, you're talking about a flyspeck, a *nothing.* And it was freshman year. Maybe it was even before Dale came aboard, and before Gruen, too. That summer Dale got a full scholarship to McGill and we fell out of touch. Gradually."

She knew what had started her off in this direction. It had been Ned's mentioning that he'd phoned his brother.

She said, "I know you considered yourself feminists, all of you, and we've talked about this, too, but there were no women in your group."

Ned laughed. "No sane woman ever wanted to be in on our nonsense. Or only one woman did, and I don't know how sane she was, and that was Claire. At Halloween she bought a fancy harlequin costume and after Halloween she wanted to go around with us, wearing it. Nobody was amused and she implied it was sexism but she got over it."

Nina said, "I think we can go now. Don't be mad at me."

"I won't," Ned said.

The descent was harder than the ascent had been. The whole thing had been too strenuous for her. A nice thing about the forest was that there was always something handy to sit on. She found a stump for them, and pulled Ned down to sit next to her. She realized that only one of his buttocks had made it onto the stump, but they weren't going to be there long. Their minds were on divergent tracks. She could feel it.

There was something she wanted to say that she couldn't. She had to know everything about him. The reason behind it was innocent, but she couldn't tell him because he would think it was emasculating and possibly it was. She was afraid of something bursting out from the cracks in the past and destroying everything. She was trying to protect an arrangement, a consummation, she'd thought she was never going to have. So she needed to know everything and there was nothing he could do.

"What is this CYO you're murmuring about?" she asked Ned.

"I didn't know I was. It's the Catholic Youth Organization. Don was important in it as a kid. I loathed going."

She thought, Get him a beautiful notebook like Joris's as a surprise.

"I'm going to get you a notebook like Joris's for your birthday," she said.

"No, don't. His is a bound book and you have to tear pages out and that fucks it."

"Okay."

He tore a page out of his spiral-bound memo notebook, crushed it into a pellet, and put it into his pocket. He said, "You know what that was? It was about a competition we had that ended up in a tie between *The Lovo-maniacs* by Rona Barrett and *The Cypresses Believe in God* by a Spaniard whose name I forget. It was about what was the dumbest novel title ever. It doesn't fit with what Gruen has to come up with."

Nina said, "You know what *you're* going to say, I guess."

"I think so."

"That's good. It's tomorrow."

There were still things she needed to tell him, things she knew, but only one of them was in any way uplifting, and even it came with a disagreeable surround. The good news was that he could forget about the Hare Krishnas wanting to be in the Convergence. Somebody had talked to a receptionist of theirs, not an official person, and it was all a misunderstanding. The bad news part was that Elliot had complained about messages coming through his communications Wurlitzer for Ned, and for her. Somebody had taken down a message from Ma, who wanted her to be sure to save the unusual bug she had found on her pillow in case it needed to be checked out. And the other piece of news she had was that in her detections she'd come across a letter from the Program Against Micronutrient Malnutrition with a six-month-old bounced check Douglas had sent them stapled to it.

"What is to be done?" Ned said softly.

"We need to be cheery," she said. He was leaking anxiety all over the place.

"What is to be done?" he said again.

"Oh Ned, you just do your best is what needs to be done. You've done enough free-associating about the meaning of life and you need to just go with something you're satisfied to say."

"That's what you see me doing. The meaning of life is the subject I hate most, unfortunately. And by the way in one of the last emails I got from Douglas he quoted something about the meaning of life. It was the philosophy of a young Frenchwoman quoted in a book on contemporary French culture he was recommending. Anyway, the girl said, *For me the meaning of life consists in the ability to meet new people.*"

"I used to feel something like that when I was very young and first left home and was meeting a bunch of new people."

"Okay . . ."

"I was still looking for you, I guess, all unknowing."

"I am not the meaning of anyone's life."

"Well of course you are."

"Please stop helping me, Nina."

"Okay, I will. But I just want to say that your friend Joris is a lovely man and he told me a sad story. Douglas called him late at night, one night, almost morning, to tell him a nightmare. This happened when Hume was about twelve and things had already gone to hell between them. The boy was standing up to his ankles in a shallow pond, wearing a plaid bathrobe that had been a favorite item from his toddler days. But it was a dream, so even though he was older, the tiny robe fit. In fact, they'd called him Little Captain Bathrobe when he was two. Anyway, the boy is standing there, turning around when his father calls out to him, and then turning away and refusing to look at his father again. That was the nightmare. So the man was suffering over his son, which we know already." What this story would add to Ned's quality of life was zero, but she'd felt she had to be free of it.

She wasn't helping Ned.

She said, "Sitting here in the gloaming. It's nice."

"It isn't gloaming yet," Ned said.

40 A sprinkling of lights showed in the manse. She liked it better where they were, at the edge of the woods.

Traveling on the bus, she had passed by a dead lake with limbless dead trees standing in it. It had looked like a gargantuan bed of nails. They would pass it again on the way home. Leaving would be a pleasure.

A dilapidated arrangement of trellises half-enclosed an especially noble old tree, doubtless to protect it. She studied her husband. She felt like pressing him up against the tree, so she did, careful not to be abrupt about it. She kissed him. She pushed a hand through his silly curly hair. What she wanted to tell him, she couldn't tell him. Later she might try to. She thought, It's simple. Ned thinks Douglas was sui generis and that he himself is a type, he, Ned, a type . . . he and the others too, but if I tell him that *he's* the sui generis one he won't believe me. She pulled Ned's hand under her sweater and blouse and onto her belly. His hand was cold. When she was more pregnant he was going to love her breasts, and then later he wouldn't, when they fell, but she would do something about it. This I vow, she thought.

She wouldn't mind visiting this place again, when it was less like a saturated sponge, say in a hot June or July, with her offspring along. Maybe *two* offsprings. She reminded herself to do some research on baby carriers.

She pushed Ned's hand down into her crotch. She just

wanted his hand present, nothing more. He knew that. He was sensitive. She didn't believe in healing touch or any of that, but his hand on her neck was definitely analgesic sometimes, if she had a headache. She was lubricating. She pulled his hand up and gave it back to him.

Some things are pleasant, she thought. She was thinking of the rustic moon bridge that would take them back onto the estate proper. It crossed the brook that spilled into the gorge where Douglas had met his death. Other brooks fed into it lower down.

She saw something else she thought was pleasant. Across the lawn she could make out Gruen and Joris strolling, their arms across one another's shoulders. It was bonhomie pure and simple. Her impression was that they had been drinking, but still it was pleasant to see.

41 He loved it when she lubricated. He hadn't been trying to get there but it had happened and it was nice and he loved her sweetmeats . . .

An inner alarm went off. Sweetmeats had been his term for Claire's labia, and it was one thing she hadn't objected to when he said it although she'd had a strict list of things never to say during sex, a rather comprehensive list. He had never said sweetmeats to Nina and if he introduced the word she would know like an arrow that it was something from his time with another woman, and she would know it was Claire and she would hate it. It wasn't exactly like calling out a former lover's name during intercourse but it was in the vicinity. Labia, the little devils, were like nothing else on the outside of the body. He could use any endearments he felt like with crazy Nina, his Soft Gem.

Ned said, "Let's be sure to get to the mess hall before they run out of frankfurters."

Nina said, "It's impossible to get hold of Elliot to talk. He's never around. And when he's around he's always slipping off." Nina was lingering on the moon bridge and it was making Ned nervous. The infrastructure around this place seemed to need attention anywhere you looked. He motioned her to join him on the other side and she did.

Ned said, "Well, I can tell you something historical about Elliot and his disappearances but my guess is you won't think it's funny. It has to do with flatulence and only men think flatulence is comical."

"Okay get it overwith."

"When we were all rooming together on Second Avenue it became evident that Elliot had a flatulence problem and he was sensitive about it. He would leave the room for no particular reason we knew of until we figured out what it was. He was sparing us. We witnessed a mortifying thing at a party in a ballroom in Midtown when Elliot slipped off and discreetly farted, away from the crowd, into a column of drapes, safely, he thought, but hiding behind the drapes was a couple kissing and they burst out into the room thinking they'd been the victims of a practical joke. Elliot went to an internist and it got better. I'm just reminiscing. Expressing gas isn't the explanation for his absences now."

"They posted the menu, you know. Maybe he's afraid of the chili."

"The problem was lactose."

Dinner wasn't until seven, so there was time for a nap.

Nina seemed not to be interested, saying, "You take a nap. I have some things to do."

All this was coming to an end. She was a force of nature and there was nothing he was going to try to do about it.

Their paths diverged. He went his way, yawning.

42 Ned was late getting down to dinner. It was the same mob scene it had become. At first he didn't see Nina. He joined the tail of the buffet queue. And then he did see her, standing with Joris and Gruen, who seemed to be watching people eat, rather than eating, themselves. Something seemed to be wrong. Both of them were holding capacious wineglasses, half-filled. Joris's eyes were funny. Nina looked unhappy. She had something to tell him. He hoped she had eaten.

Nina joined him. She'd had dinner. She said Joris and Gruen hadn't.

Gesturing at the two, she said, "They're *happy*, both of them. That's what my mother called it."

"Let me get something."

He filled a plate for himself, concentrating on vegetables. He had no appetite. From a distance, Jacques raised a drumstick to him.

He didn't like what he was seeing, with his friends, but he didn't know what he was seeing. He sat down in a chair and ate half of the rice and eggplant mélange he'd taken. Nina wanted him to do something.

She disposed of his plate, and said, "I would like to get them out of here."

"First, let's get some coffee."

She was impatient. "Maybe I can get them to take some coffee outside. I had a struggle getting Joris to leave the bar. Let me see if they'll go for it. Joris is very upset. Very. The thing is, he's spoiling for a scene. He's talking about going home."

She left for the dessert station and organized four cups of coffee on a tray. They would all go outside. They would walk down to the bridge, whose understructure was being reinforced.

Work was going on at the bridge across the brook on the road up from the Vale. Cables were being wound around the two main stanchions. Watching it happen would be something to do. The workers, four of them, were wet and unhappy. The temperature was dropping. They were cursing the torrent they had to work in and out of. They moderated their language after noticing Nina there. Blindingly bright floodlights illuminated the scene.

Nina pushed two empty tool chests together to make seating. Joris definitely needed to sit down. In adolescence Nina had been told she was hypoglycemic and she had gotten into the habit of carrying backup snacks around with her, tight little foil packets of nuts, cheeses, crackers, dried fruits. Her condition had gone away but the habit of arming herself against potential gaps in the availability of appropriate food had persisted. Just in general, she always seemed to have needful things with her, like aspirin or Neo-Synephrine. Nina had succeeded in inducing Joris to finish one of the tall paper cups of coffee she had secured for them and now he was eating a roll, in a gingerly way, but eating it. Joris and Nina had their backs to the glare of the work lights. What Ned wanted to do *at that moment* was say something to Nina like *I would always like to be what I am now, with you.*

Gruen wanted a word aside with Ned. Together they stepped away from the lights.

Gruen said, "Joris wants to go home. I talked to him, but he still wants to. I wouldn't mind leaving either, but I think we should all be here. You need to talk to him."

Ned said, "Isn't there a story called 'The Runaway Pallbearers'? This isn't good. He needs to be here, too."

Ned was having a particularly strong reaction to the idea of Joris leaving. Partly it was selfish because he hadn't finished the task of putting together what they had all been, with what they were now. And the question was still there of whether their true interior selves—the subtle bodies inside—were still there and functioning despite what age and accident and force of circumstance may have done to hurt them. He meant something like that . . . that when they had become friends it had been a friendship established between *subtle bodies,* by which he meant *the ingredients* of what they were to be . . .

He was succeeding in being confused by his thoughts and feeling strongly about them at the same time. This was about what you loved in a friend as a friend. He loved something in Elliot, still. Maybe there was a window in life and then it closed. Nina was asking him if he was all right. He wasn't, because none of this could be said, really. But there was that window, before anybody had accomplished anything to speak of, when the *ingredients,* by which he meant the subtle bodies, shone their light. Douglas was only the first of the friends to die. Everything connected with him was foreclosed now, Ned thought. But there are four of us left, and if this is too mystical fuck it . . . I sound like Ma and Ma sounds like Madame Blavatsky . . . but so mote it be and fuck it.

Unexpectedly, Joris came up to them in the darkness. For a moment he seemed unsteady on his feet, but only for a moment.

"I love your wife," Joris said to Ned, who came back with, "Watch yourself."

The three men sighed heavily in unison, noticed it, and laughed together. Nina was walking toward them.

"Joris wants to abandon us," Ned said to Nina.

"I hope he won't," she said. Ned sensed something hollow in her words. He was puzzled.

"We await his words, my dear." That was the wrong tone. Everything was delicate.

Joris squared his shoulders and locked his hands behind his back. He said, "I don't want to say anything tomorrow and I want to leave."

Ned said, "Why?"

Joris said, "Here's the why. Why is because the world is a machine that *works*. It even improves itself. Douglas didn't know that. And we didn't know that."

This was peculiar. Joris was normally an excellent drunk, if that was the way to put it. This was more than just the wine speaking. There had been a personal event, or a philosophical one, something.

Ned said, "Wait a minute. Something's going on. And you're not saying the world is perfect as is, I take it. That ideology . . ." Joris shook his head over-vigorously. There was a silence.

Ned continued, "So Joris, what is this? Is it something you just realized? *What?* Go ahead. Talk."

Joris said, "We have this thing, evolution. S'okay . . . and we have *us*, this nasty primate. S'okay we have this nasty primate who keeps trying to build an order . . . a safe order different from the beast world only there are problems. Because the male part of the species goes insane over three things, just like the other animals. It goes crazy over those three things, which are sex, death, and goods. Or say money. Or say status, which money is for.

"S'okay by evolution of course we are talking about social evolution. And social evolution plays around and finds an antidote for the fear of death, which is religion, the churches, the sects, all that. And it keeps opening up in new forms like a perennial. And they don't pay taxes, we subsidize it. They all deny death and the people are happy. Religion helps them, most of them, and that keeps it rolling."

Ned said, "Come on, what does this have to do with you leaving? You're drunk. There's a damned *memorial* tomorrow. We can talk about these cosmic issues after it's over."

Nina said, "Maybe he should just talk now. It isn't going to be too long, is it, Joris?"

"*No it's not.* S'okay, take sex, where the males happen to want to fuck anybody they feel like. Somebody has to keep the babies coming and raise them up. Evolution tries lots of things. Religion helps but not as much as it did, with death, which I said before. Sorry. So . . . okay, social evolution gives us easy divorces, serial marriages, okay to be a single mother, pat yourself on the back.

"Money. Greed, easy. Capitalism! The universal raffle! Overhead to be paid, of course, unemployment insurance . . ."

Nina said, "Joris, that's enough for now. The things you

really want to say you can't say tonight. You'll explain it all tomorrow. After the memorial. But you have to stay."

Ned said to Nina, "What is he saying? I guess I'm tired. Is he saying that Douglas didn't have this big world machine concept he's giving us? Why are we even talking about this? Look. Douglas had an *attitude* that looked like an *idea*, to us. We were children. Now he's dead and here we are."

Nina, Ned, and Gruen all said they wanted to go, but Joris insisted on checking the progress of the work gang at the bridge. They went with him.

43 Ned wondered what was going on. Nina had been next door for almost an hour, and then talking in the corridor with Gruen. It was time to sleep. He wanted the day to be over, but he knew she was containing some news for him. And there was something he wanted to say.

She came into the room. He held up his hand before she could start to speak. Ned said, "I want to explain that thing with Joris. You have to see it as more like a seizure than like an epiphany or a theory he was presenting. I've been there before with Joris, drinking, both of us. When he's drunk he's like that. He'll be fine tomorrow."

Nina said, "I know, I know. And I have a lot to tell you but I want to take up something *really important* first, to wit, would you ever say I have a *short* face? What I mean is, would that ever occur to you?"

"No, of course not. Where is this amusing question coming from?"

"Well, from Jacques. He said something I believe was a compliment but I think it translated like that."

"Unfortunately you can't believe anything the man says, my dear. And by the way did you know he's a moon-landing denier?"

"He is not. Don't make things up."

"Okay, but he might as well be."

"Oh please. He's very sympathetic. Do you know that he forged the most perfect, the most beautiful name tag, using machines or whatever they are that Douglas had? Press credentials."

"Why is he discussing your attributes?"

"Oh you mean my assets? I think he said I had a *brief* and short face, but I'm not sure. I'm taking it as a compliment. Why don't you ever tell me I have a brief and short face?"

"I'll try to remember. You think he's an outlaw, yay! and I'm not."

Nina was looking for something.

"What are you looking for?"

He couldn't quite believe that she meant it when she said she was looking for a radio to play so the sound would cover what she was going to say.

"You mean like spies?" he asked.

"*Exactement.*"

She was serious. Defeated, he joined her search for a radio and found a clock radio on a shelf in the closet. He set it on the bedside table, plugged it in, and it worked. He tuned it into something religious, in fact Pentecostal, because the preacher would occasionally break into episodes of glossolalia. She was delaying.

She said she was cold and he proposed that they get into bed together, keep their clothes on until they were warm, and *talk*. It was cool, not cold, in the room, in his opinion.

She had plenty of layers on, a denim windbreaker over a heavy sweater and tee shirt. She had on her famous boots, jeans, and a floppy black beret that might be hers or not, he didn't know. He'd noticed that the women staff seemed to be offering her articles of clothing on loan. She sat on the edge of the bed and clapped her thighs together and jammed her hands between them.

He could tell she liked the idea of getting into bed. He hoped she understood that it was not going to be a case of once more into the breach tonight. He had a headache.

"First, what I'm going to tell you is mostly just recent. Not all of it is. And I had a reason for not telling you right away.

"Which is the following. Wait a minute, I was just going to lie to you about why I've been holding on to this. Let me start over.

"I don't know. I think I didn't want to tell you all this because of the way it makes Joris look. Not sordid or anything, but not great, either. And Ned I feel I've made friends here, strange as you may think that is. I like the man. I like him the best. Or no, I like him about equally with Gruen. I have to tell you that the story is going to make some other people seem sordid, but I don't care about them.

"What I know is from Gruen . . ."

Ned said, "Please tell me what in hell this is, and why is he talking to you about it and not me?"

"If you listen you'll understand. Oh God. Well here it is. Iva about a year ago initiated a peculiar kind of affair with Joris. Yes."

Ned said, "And he told Gruen. Everybody talked to Gruen."

Nina said, "The affair was rather intermittent. Joris told

Gruen it started when she just sought him out. Joris couldn't have been more surprised. She showed up and collapsed on him in misery. First she went to his office and then came to his apartment, collapsing. She was trapped and unhappy with Douglas is what she said and a divorce was going to come and she had always felt something for Joris, i.e., was in love with him. She was saying that.

"So an affair began. Previous to the affair Joris said he had seen Douglas and Iva twice a year, tops, at dinners, events, in New York City. Joris was overwhelmed. The logistics of the affair that developed were built around a convenient historical fact—she had been going to a particular hairdresser in Manhattan for years."

Ned said, "Take your time. Get your breath."

Nina pulled off the beret. She continued, "She was definite about it. She wanted to marry him once she got divorced. It was all going to be soon.

"Now. Now. The immediate cause of the break with Douglas was that she had caught him cheating with someone in a long-distance scheme. There was a woman he would hook up with whenever they could arrange it. Both of them traveled a lot. And the worst is that Iva found out that it was a deal to get this woman—he never named her—pregnant. And it was just intolerable. He was passing it off as a favor he was doing so someone could be a single mother, or just a mother period. So he was halfway claiming it wasn't sex, it was an altruistic endeavor."

Ned thought, *Don't speculate.* But he had a hideous idea of who it might have been, must have been. His heart hurt, speculating. He coughed elaborately to get himself a break, a minute to stay sane and reliable.

Nina said, "All this came pouring out of Gruen. David.

I don't see why I shouldn't call him David. I do call him David. Because David knew about everything that had happened, he didn't want to leave, because he felt he owed it to you, and to Joris, and especially to Hume, to stay and do his best. He had only nice little stories about Hume to relate, nothing bizarre. One was at a picnic someplace, and Hume said, when a bag with three beer bottles in it was brought out, Oh the little things are trying to keep each other cold. David and Helen have no kids and he went out of his way to do things with Hume when he could.

"Really, she overwhelmed Joris. When she got to the apartment the first time she was topless under her blouse and within minutes she had dropped her coat where she stood and jerked up her blouse and mashed Joris's hands all over her magnificent breasts. And that was step one."

44 Ned was listening to Nina but he was losing some of what she was saying. She had just made a reference to Lincoln Center. He could ask her later.

Of course the individual soliciting Douglas to get pregnant had been his own Claire, who was on record with *him* as not wanting children. If the plan had worked, he would have had a baby to raise with her and would have assumed it was his, and that would have made for a life of its own kind. Nina must know it was Claire. It was kind of her not to treat it like what it was. It was going to be nothing. He was going to make it be nothing. Because it was going to be just one of the many things from his past with Claire that were going to be nothing forever. Were nothing now.

Claire was devious, so the question of whether her

game had been to get pregnant and then use that fact to get money or some unimaginable arrangement out of it from Douglas was real. Or had it been the sincere game of wanting to have Douglas's offspring because in her heart of hearts Douglas was the one she loved and revered and whose essence she wanted to reproduce? He could think of other permutations but didn't want to. He had to concentrate on his luck in escaping something profoundly wrong, and not on the insult and not on his self-esteem. Nina takes care of my self-esteem, he thought.

"You don't look like you're listening," Nina said.

"I wasn't, for a second. Now I am. It was Claire, wasn't it? In your opinion."

"Ned he didn't use the name. I think it is pretty obvious and I hate her. I hate her. Ah, don't look so hurt. Don't. You escaped something that would have gotten worse and worse. I thought of not telling you, but it would've come out because that story was the fuse burning underneath Douglas's marriage and that was what blew up and led Iva to go after Joris. Also, Ned, I wanted to be the one to tell you and not have you get it from some other source and say How could you not tell me? Say, How weak do you think I am? Say that to *me* instead, Ned."

"I have to digest this."

"*No you don't, Ned*. Or if you do, digest it. Do it. Do it now. You know I don't like to talk against her but this is more than just something to add to the wrongs she did you, my man. But now *I* have you. *You have me*."

"Claire was a feral person," Ned said.

"Perfect word."

Ned took his jacket off. He said, "Let's take our shoes off and get under the covers."

"You look cold," Nina said.

"I'm not, or just sort of, but I want to get under the covers."

Ned took her boots off for her. She reached to help him unlace his boots but he declined her help. He appreciated the offer.

"You do feel cold," she said. They got into bed and held each other.

She said, "Anyway . . ." There was more.

In a way, Ned didn't want to hear whatever more there was. But he had no choice.

Nina said, "So anyway Iva was insistent that she wanted to marry Joris. She apparently thought she could overcome his big problem, which was that he was never going to marry again for all the reasons we know. But of course she was kind of perfect. She was married, something he found attractive in women. And she was willing to work with that, including the prostitutes. She believes in herself, as you may have noticed.

"Now, what David says is that there were two parts to what was going on. Douglas was in financial ruin and Joris was rich. And she was infuriated with Douglas over his infidelity, which he refused to call it. Elliot had told her bankruptcy was coming. And Gruen—David—is sure that Iva figured she could rush Joris into marriage and then she'd be all set.

"This had been going on for eight or nine months before Joris talked about it to David, who was astounded and couldn't think of anything helpful to say so told Joris to go to a relationship counselor! Joris thought he might be falling in love. And she was hitting all the keys on the piano, saying that Hume needed a better father and blaming Douglas's numerous absences for Hume's problems. And there was *flattery* involved. David said that Iva was praising Joris for his, what did he call it, his sexual strength.

"And this was the way it was going for almost a whole year and Joris was wavering, wavering.

"But then the signals changed in some way he didn't understand. The only thing he could think of that he'd done wrong was not to promise to sign on the dotted line if she got her divorce.

"But she was turning it off. It ended with a phone call saying she had thought everything over and the affair would have to stop. She said she was very sorry, but she *couldn't go into it*. Oh, she did express *some* sadness. But that was the end and he was left with a mystery."

Ned got out of bed without explaining why. He needed to pace. He said, "That's something like the way it ended with Claire. A sudden announcement. Maybe that's getting to be standard now. Except Claire did say there was another person, which makes it not the same kind of mystery. I need to pee."

Mainly, he needed to think about something else, say, like why the French let Rodin freeze to death after they kicked him out of the storeroom he was pathetically squatting in at the Louvre and what about his friends who promised to send coal?

"I didn't pee," he said.

"What?"

"I couldn't. There is someone in the bathroom taking a shower who doesn't answer."

"Oh for God's sake."

Ned looked around the room. There were his petitions. There were plenty of people on the premises he should bring petitions to. But he had no heart for it.

"You could go downstairs. Or if you move the bed a little, you can pee out the window."

"No, I'll just wait for Godot to get finished in there."

"Well sit down. I'm not quite through talking anyway. But first I want to say that I hate it that they're serving these heirloom tomatoes."

"Why? They're delicious."

"That's why. Because when you go back to regular tomatoes it's like eating with plastic silverware."

"Thank you for trying to help me. You are a dear person. Say what you wanted to say."

"Okay, Ned. So the situation just sits there for a few months. And then death takes Douglas. Joris feels vile even thinking it, but he wonders if it means anything for him and Iva. He's probably thinking of sex more than marriage, but he's still angry, and kind of messed up and thinking about her. So then comes the summons to the group. He shows up, and here we all are, and hark, the shower just turned off. Go and come back."

He was more grateful to her than he could say. She was trying everything, but he was dropping inward.

Ned said, "I know you want me to get into bed, but I feel like not doing it. I'll just sit here."

He could see that she was trying to proceed brightly with him. She was sitting up. She said, "Well you know you're welcome to sit on the end of the bed as long as you like, but it's warmer under the covers.

"So back to my adventures—and try to look interested—I was stirring up the ashes in the downstairs fireplace in the tower and there were a few intact edges of pages that had been burned there, enough so I could tell that the typescript was about fringe science stuff of the kind he was interested in. The magnetic poles are going to reverse in case you've forgotten. And I found one whole page on the sun getting dimmer. So then I had the idea to go upstairs. I still can't get my breath, wait a minute . . .

"I look at that row of binders on his shelf, all empty, and my guess is that somebody wanted to get rid of the exotic science because it's embarrassing. After Douglas died I think somebody got rid of this mass of science fiction and Elliot has been saying the plan was to publish all his social science writings of which there were plenty. And it was going to be under the heading Unde Malum, which means where does evil come from. What do you think of me?"

He said, "The same thing I always think." But he was dead, sitting there.

45 Help him, Nina thought. She had to get him away from himself. But she also needed to *keep calm*. Maybe it was ridiculous but it felt like she was pregnant, in fact *he* was acting like she was pregnant more than she was herself. She had to do something. She was afraid of momentum. And momentum meant an episode of shock and humiliation taking hold and rolling and rolling and rolling and you can only watch.

She had to do something. He was not going to be interested in sex tonight, not in the state he was in.

"Listen," she said. But then nothing came to her. There
had to be something to distract him. The racket coming
from under their wing of the house was less, if she wasn't
mistaken. She had gotten to like it, it was soporific, like
ValueVision. He was just sitting there in a slumped state she
couldn't bear. Once Ned had talked about maybe losing it
and collapsing all the way down and then joking that then
he could become a motivational speaker and make a million, which wasn't that funny.

He had to be all right. She wanted to grow old with him
and she didn't care if growing old meant shuffling around
in a house that could be neater and looking for things and
shouting over and over *What?* She thought, *I embrace the
end.*

Someone was knocking at the door. *Not now,* she
thought.

Ned looked wildly at her. He was shaking his head.

She went to the door. It was Jacques. He was being
decently circumspect and apologetic. He handed her a
damp towel and a sheaf of papers and withdrew, thanking
her.

46 He knew she was doing her best. She was bringing light into dark places. It would be fine, later
on. He would be fine. Gene Gene made a machine, Joe Joe
made it go, Doug Doug pulled the plug, he thought. He was
regressing and it was counterproductive and he had to stop.

Nina said, "Have regular facial expressions." That was

a command from their inventory of facetious devices they used to josh one another out of bad moods. She would put on a chicken suit if it would make him laugh.

Nina got out of bed. She removed her jeans and sweater. She worked her bra off under the tee shirt. She would sleep in that and her panties. She waited for him. She shook the bedcovers in a way she hoped was inviting. Down to his briefs, Ned got in with her.

Nina turned on her side to face him and said, "I'm sorry but I have more to tell you."

"Why am I here?" he asked no one. He meant several things. One was why he was giving this time to his meaningless personal history when the country was getting ready to burn people to death in large numbers. The mental volume of the thought had been equivalent to a shout. That was odd. He was screaming at himself, it seemed. His personal history would amount to nothing, would amount to a surplus of painful feelings worth nothing, in the balance. And another thing, he had been a fuckwit. His documented stupidity was set in stone for the friends he loved, still loved, to put into the balance when they thought of him. And *another* thing. Why hadn't somebody kept him up to date? But he knew the answer to that and it was because it was unimaginable for either of them, Joris or Gruen, to tell him man to man. No, it was the accidental availability of Nina. If she hadn't been there, what he was to Claire would have remained secret, apparently. His thoughts were killing him.

He got out of bed without explanation. He needed to move around while he was suffering.

"What else is there?" he asked.

Nina said, "Well this is from Jacques. Who got it off the

Réseau Voltaire, which is on the internet. It's an aggregator site. How do you like my pronunciation?"

Ned made an aggrieved sound, but motioned to her to continue.

She said, "The story is that Douglas made a critical discovery that I don't understand. It sounds really technical to me and I don't know how much he knew about advanced optics, etcetera, but apparently he did, because what he invented or discovered was the answer to a problem that had been unsolved all during the rise of digital reproduction . . . which as you know very well is the problem of distinguishing between real and fake in digital images and products. Every intelligence service in the world was working on it, according to my source, Jacques. By the way, there's all sorts of complicated equipment in the tower basement. Jacques says that Douglas was negotiating with the Mossad to give the thing to them and they would use it jointly with the CIA, but he wanted to be taken care of forever, if you get my drift. And it was important that no evidence of the transfer, such as a sale or big payments to him that could be traced, would ever surface. And listen to this. The sheer existence of the invention if that's what it was had to be kept secret. It was going to be worked out through foundations in Germany and Israel. Money would go for some kind of institute for forensic justice. I told you about the similar thing that had been done for him earlier for some lesser service or discovery where he got paid a staggering fee for the *Tambov* movie script. Someone named Bondarchuk was involved. That payment to Douglas was called a pass-through . . ."

She was leaning down and feeling along the floor near

the bed. She found her boots. She threw first one and then the other at him, not hard, at his knees. He had almost no reaction.

"Please come back to bed," she said, raising her voice. He sighed and obeyed. He wanted her to finish her presentation so that the sermonizing on the radio could end forever.

Nina took his hand. "There's not much more to tell. The deal over his invention was on and then it was off. There was constant negotiation going on. The invention was never patented because that would show the thing existed. The deal looked like it was off, I guess, when Iva was after Joris. But who knows? And then it was on again and then suddenly Douglas was dead, out of it, unable to go out and promote himself and this new institute, so now there's this public relations spectacular. Which is really all it is, but you'd figured that out. So now tell me what you think."

"I don't know if it's true," Ned said.

"Neither do I, but it's what I've been told and it's credible to me."

Ned covered his face with the blanket briefly. He lowered it and said, "I think I'm not going to have an opinion on this. It's a pretty good example of a fait accompli. We were talking about that the other day. If Douglas came up with something you can use to defend the better countries against the worse countries, fine. We can never make it up to the Jews, anyway, Americans can't. It goes back to the beginning, beginnings. Benjamin Franklin wanted to deny Jews citizenship. Roosevelt's policymaker on Jewish refugees from Germany was a horrible anti-Semite. So you might say, Well, his invention is defensive except when it isn't. That's true. I'm making the decision to be okay with it if it's half defensive, half something dark. Nobody will leave the Israelis alone. It's a fight in the Convergence. It's the Palestinians we're supposed to be for, first of all, but the Palestinians won't leave the Israelis alone and remember how everybody at the Labor Center was outraged when the Israelis started putting up their great walls because they were tired of being blown up in their cafés? Everybody said it was an outrage but voilà the bombings stopped. The Palestinians had grievances *in spades* but they fought back like . . . like monsters. I know it's not simple, but that's all I have to say."

He could tell that there was something else she wanted to say to him.

"Do you remember the first joke you made to me when we were dating, or not even dating, when we were still in the taste-exchanging phase and you asked me what kind of movies I liked and I don't remember what I said. And then you asked what kind I *didn't* like and I said, westerns, violence, and suspense, and you said, Does that mean you don't want to go with me to see *Kill the Horse Slowly*?"

He said, "I'm not sleeping in my underwear no matter what you say." He got out of bed, went to the chest of drawers, opened it, and took out a pair of pajamas and held them up for her to see.

He said, "These may be Douglas's pajamas but I don't care. Tonight I'm wearing them."

She said, "Ned, you're funny."

"I once was."

47 Ned couldn't sleep. Nina's penlight was under her pillow. He extracted it with care, managing not to disturb her. There were the papers Jacques had handed Nina earlier. They were on the floor next to the bed. Thinking about the old days was difficult, tonight. It was like looking at events through a dark mist. I hear as through a wall, poorly, one of them had said once. Certain times had been amusing. Like Douglas's impromptu heckling of the Venceremos Brigade reunions in Washington Square Park. Douglas thought Castro was a clown and he referred to Cuba as the Brave Little Police State. Ned remembered it all, Douglas shouting *Páredon!*, the cry the Cuban rebels used in their salad days when they were sending their enemies to the firing squad. And of course by the seventies the volunteer sugar-cane-cutter brigadiers had forgotten what the word means and just took Douglas as encouraging them when in fact he was both reminding them of something shameful and insinuating subtly that they themselves could go to the wall, for all he cared. Douglas's mind had been a dungheap of the left's past transgressions, which had gone well with his occasional appearances as the conscience of the left, or one of them, anyway.

Jacques was obviously trying to help him. And obviously Nina had let Jacques know about his trouble with the encomium for tomorrow. It wasn't Jacques's fault that he got his information from a stream, the internet, that ran alongside a membrane that only let bits of it through into the mainstream media flow. There was truth on both sides of the membrane.

Jacques had done some work on the internet, for him. Jacques was all right. He had printed out a poem, "Men on Earth," by Robert Desnos. Nina would know who Robert Desnos was. He read the poem.

Men on Earth

There were four of us at a table
Drinking red wine and singing
When we felt like it.

A wallflower fades in a garden gone to seed
The memory of a dress at the bend of an avenue
Venetian blinds beating against a sash.

The first man says: "The world is wide and the wine is fine
Wide is my heart and fine my blood
Why are my hands and my heart so empty?"

A summer evening the chant of rowers on a river
The reflection of huge poplars
And the foghorn from a tug requesting passage.

The second man says: "I discovered a fountain
The water was fresh and sweet-smelling
I no longer know where it is and all four of us are dying."

How beautiful are the streams in small towns
On an April morning
When they carry rainbows along

Subtle Bodies

The third man says: "We were born a short time ago
And already we have more than a few memories
Though I want to forget them."

A stairway full of shadow
A door left ajar
A woman surprised naked.

The fourth man says: "What memories?
This moment we are camped
And my friends we are going to leave one another."

Night falls on a crossroad
The first light in the fields
The odor of burning grass.

We left each other, all four of us
Which one was I and what did I say?
It was a long time ago.

The glistening rump of a horse
The cry of a bird in the night
The rippling of water under a bridge.

One of the four is dead

This was a poem he wasn't going to finish. He dropped
the pages.

48 Nina woke up and saw that Ned was getting dressed. She watched. It would be more accurate to say that he was getting dressed and re-dressed. She didn't know if it was a mania, exactly, but he was in some state completely new to her regarding the way he looked. He had collected and laid out different elements to choose from for the outfit he was going to present himself in today. It was very strange. He had assembled a collection of shirts gotten presumably from Joris and Elliot, maybe some of Douglas's, from Iva—Gruen's shirts wouldn't fit Ned—and one shirt that he needn't have bothered with, a pale floral print. He must have been out scouring the world for shirts since sunrise.

The radio was on, low. She concentrated. It was the local news.

She said, "Me oh my, another pedophile running a summer camp, apparently the woods are full of them."

She thought, There is no handbook on the subject of how you help people who are acting crazy.

It was only seven and Ned had showered and shaved. Ned was someone who needed to wash his hair every day and he hadn't been doing that. His curly hair looked vital when it had just been washed, not electrical exactly, but springing up and lively and nice. He had shaved hard, which is what he called shaving scrupulously and not in his usual nominal way. He was turning his head from side to side in front of the mirror over the chest of drawers, so he could check his gleaming cheeks.

The tie he was holding up against the front of an unfamiliar tan shirt was one she had seen Joris wear. It was purple. He would never wear it.

The house was full of nuts, by which she meant that somebody kept refilling the little bowls of cashews and almonds etcetera distributed around the common rooms. Men loved nuts. Ned was munching them all day there. He's gained a little weight, she thought, in this house. Ma had given her a piece of advice she had paid attention to, but she could only put it into effect when she was in control of the eating environment. It was: restrict the kinds of nuts you keep in your house to the kind in shells so they can't be consumed by the fistful, because cracking them constitutes an obstacle that keeps consumption down and makes noise so you can always rush in from someplace else in the house when you hear it and distract your husband with a stick of celery.

Ned said, "I like this."

Nina said, "It shits. You are not going to appear in a purple tie! The black one is perfect. It's perfect for a funeral. You like the purple one because it's matte, and you think the black one is too shiny for a proletarian like you, *but this is a funeral*, Mister Bakunin."

He said, "Okay, then. This is going to be it." He had gotten into the black jeans he'd brought with him. Someone on the staff had pressed them to a fare-thee-well. He slipped his borrowed black suit jacket on and for some reason draped the black tie in an X across his chest, signifying that it was provisional. He inhaled and held his breath while she graded him. Men always do that, she thought.

"You look marvelous," she said, realizing just after the fact that she was resurrecting a tag line from *Saturday Night*

Live and her long durance vile with Bob. She thanked whatever gods may be that she hadn't said it with the ellipses between the three words that made the phrase comical, or pronounced the "mar" in marvelous as "mah."

"Okay then," he said again.

She didn't really like the way he was sounding. It was tight. Or it was going from tight to less tight through sheer self-control. It was her opinion that life should feel like something other than falling down an endless flight of stairs. Maybe a solid breakfast would help him. He'd only eaten a little rice and eggplant for dinner.

She said, "In my role as warden of your public self, I want to see your nails."

He came toward her, the backs of his hands held out. His nails were clipped. She liked his hands.

"How am I?" he asked.

"You're darling."

"No, you know what I mean."

"You are completely fine. But you need to relax. In fact, why don't you do the breathing exercise you're always, well not always, occasionally, telling me to do, in and out, out and hold, that one."

She threw the covers back while Ned performed the breathing exercise.

When he spoke to her he sounded worse. He said, "By the way, just so you know, the celebrities are all eating their meals separately, not with us in the mess hall."

"They are?"

"Yes, and there's a Nazi hunter in the house. Not Wiesenthal but his deputy or somebody. Gruen will want to talk to him, but won't be in the same room, malheureusement. Jacques is affecting my life."

Nina said, "What about that poem. Was the poem any good?"

Ned sighed heavily. "I can't use it. I'll thank him, though."

He said, "I feel like kissing you. I could never kiss Claire in the morning until she'd brushed her teeth."

"*I beg you not to bring her up unnecessarily. I beg you.*"

"Right."

Nina said, "I think that shirt's fine because it's good quality, but I have to get cuff links somewhere. Somebody will have some."

4 9 Ned's mind was everywhere. He hadn't decided on what he was going to do re the memorial. Keep smiling, he thought.

He had eaten more for breakfast than he'd intended to, at Nina's urging. Gruen appeared next to him at the coffee urn. He was looking for Nina and Ned explained that she had gone to find a bathroom without a line in front of it and cuff links.

Gruen asked, "Have you seen the program?"

Ned shook his head. Gruen said, "Well, we're not on it by name. We're in a segment called, quite simply, *Voices!*"

"No kidding. But I'm not surprised. Yes I am, actually. And may I say *you* look nice."

Gruen was wearing a black cardigan and Ned wanted to tell him he should unbutton it because it was too tight on him, but there was no point in that. It would just make him uncomfortable and the borrowed shirt was probably too tight, too. His black tie wasn't shiny and he had gotten

decent unconspicuous cuff links to close his French cuffs.
If Nina didn't find something he'd borrow a stapler and
shut the flapping things with that. He looked around at the
crowd disconsolately. He asked Gruen if he'd met any interesting guests lately. "There are thousands to choose from,"
Ned said.

Supposedly Nina had gone to scout out someplace at
one of the tables but he saw that instead she was engaged in
conversation with frère Jacques. Joris was not in evidence,
and Gruen had lost track of him. The media component of
the crowd had swollen and Ned was seeing faces now and
then that were faintly familiar.

"Doesn't this make you feel minor?" Ned asked Gruen,
who shrugged.

"I have to get Nina. Are those your cuff links?" Ned
asked.

"No, I got them from Joris. He brought a couple of
pairs, but he's using the others."

"Where's the nearest stapler, do you suppose?" Ned
said.

Gruen said, "I'm going to make a scrambled egg sandwich on one of those delicious rolls. I'll scoop the eggs off
the top because on the bottom they're dried out. I'll make
you one if you want. I was about to say we can eat standing
up, but there's room for three or four at that table."

"I've eaten, but Nina hasn't. We'll sit with you. Let me
go detach her from the French," Ned said. Ned forged his
way to Nina's side.

Jacques looked particularly unkempt. He had shaved
carelessly and what looked like popped white stitching ran
along the rim of his lower lip. Earlier Ned had seen Nina
draw a circle with her finger around her own lips, which had

made Ned nervous, but now it was clear that what she had been doing was innocent, of course. Jacques was wearing a black tee shirt and for some reason a black headband.

They all sat down with Gruen. Jacques served the coffee. It was pleasant.

Somebody had to find Joris.

50 Nina asked Ned where else they should go to look for Joris. They'd asked Iva, who'd had no idea. They'd sensed something odd in Iva's manner, since the day before—a sea change, a suggestion of jubilance.

Elliot had nothing to impart about Joris's whereabouts, and he, also, had seemed distinctly more relaxed. Nina was puzzled. Ned couldn't think about it that much because he needed to talk to her about his encomium problem, and immediately.

They were standing behind the manse in a spot Nina liked. It was beside a hillock with a young cedar on top. It was fragrant there.

He had asked her earlier if he looked okay and she had said that he looked perfect, very funereal, and had reminded him to stand up straight and *keep* standing up straight. The cuff links he was wearing were courtesy of the excellent Nadine Rose.

The line *His mind more jury than judge* came to him from someplace in world literature. He told Nina that he still couldn't decide what he was going to talk about at the memorial.

"I realize that, and I wish you'd come up with an outline at least. I'm afraid you have in your head the idea that you're going to approach this with nothing in your mind but a great cloud of unknowing and that out of that is going to come inspiration and some perfect utterance. Well, maybe . . . anyway, this doesn't start until four thirty, so we have plenty of time, if you want my help."

"I could start with, say, A toast to Zeus, the protector of friendships." He waited for her reply. She was going to be kind.

Nina said, "I think . . . you can do better. Zeus is kind of embarrassing."

Ned wanted to go someplace else, but he didn't know where. Nina was always trying to help him and he appreciated it. She thought he was too easy on his staff at work, Derek in particular. He remembered what she'd said, mocking him, when she'd been urging him to get on Derek's case: Um, Derek, if you're not busy, may I bother you for a minute to ask could you maybe try and be at least a little bit less half-assed now and then in the future?

He liked being around the hillock with the cedar and he realized it reminded him of the last scene in *The Seven Samurai* with the burial mounds of the three dead heroes marked with their swords.

Earlier they had seen a hearse parked in front of the manse, delivering Douglas's ashes. The sense that they were witnessing the evolution of a gigantic machine came over Ned. A vast party tent had been erected.

Nina took his hand. She said, "I want you to promise me that if you're ever depressed you'll tell me."

"What's this about?"

"Nothing, I just wanted to say that. I don't want you to . . . I don't know."

They decided to walk down and inspect the tent.

Nina said, "And promise me you'll forget about toasts. What will you do, hold up an imaginary glass? This isn't a banquet . . ."

"I'm not arguing, you notice."

Nina said, "Your friend David is very smart and they should have made *him* talk about Douglas's philosophy, so called, not you. Do you know what he said about Douglas? He said Douglas's mind was for bizarro ideas what a belfry is for bats."

"That isn't entirely fair. Anyway . . ." He trailed off. "I want to say something substantive."

He felt like embracing her, so he did. They leaned against one another and it was pleasant in the breeze, in the sun. He was thinking that in the future somebody was going to be designated to do for him something like what he was supposed to do for Douglas. If that happened anytime soon it would be too soon. He had more to do with his life.

51 Nina was feeling acutely that she had to guide him and leave him alone at the same time. She could well imagine him crafting something that would relate heavily to his own faults as a friend. He was subject to guilt, attacks of it. He could also come up with the most far fucking fetched candidates for empathy, like an old friend who had circulated a hostile, invented, story involving them, to their astonishment. But Ned felt sorry for her *because of the guilt he was certain she must feel!*—so he wouldn't mortify her by making an issue of it.

And *now* he was wracking his brain for a way to publicly praise his friend, his old friend, the monstrous Douglas.

Outside the tent were ranks of folding chairs. Ned decided to borrow two of them. He carried the chairs down the slope past the death gorge and set them up in an odd enclosure. Someone had created a rough circle of corkscrew topiary boxwood plants in wooden tubs. They were doubtless destined to be moved to some less inscrutable location, but for now, it amused him to sit down with Nina in this askew setting.

He began again immediately with his dilemma, talking fast. He said, "Well I had the idea of beginning by shouting a parture to the crowd. Everything has a history . . . Douglas got a certain satisfaction out of fishing up lacunae in the English language, so there was a game called Filling in the White Spaces in the Dictionary—"

Nina interrupted him. "When you said start by shouting something, I thought, For Christ's sake he's talking about that Great Pan Is Dead idea which is the dumbest fucking thing I ever heard of. And by the way, what is a parture?"

"No no no, not that. And partures was the antonym Douglas invented for greetings. He said that a single word for the business of taking leave was missing in English, so we had our own, partures. One was *Peace to Your Loins!* Also *Watch the Skies!* And . . ."

"*No!*" Nina shouted, deeply agitated. She made as if to get to her feet but he restrained her, overwhelming her distress with insistences that the idea wasn't a serious one, it was just something he remembered.

She said, "*Well don't yell things out as though they're hilarious or something. They aren't.* Not even *faintly.* They're *very annoying.*"

"And then we did another thing when we went our separate ways, slapping and punching each other and shouting *Basta!* as though we were Sicilians disgusted with one another."

"*Are you trying to drive me completely insane?*"

Ned said, "No. Really. Just thinking about things that happened."

Nina thought, I have to be more directive, it can't be helped and time is passing and he's lost, still. She said, "So now before you say anything else let's get it clear we are leaving Iraq out of it, okay? People are here for a very specific purpose which is to remember Douglas, a complicated person who was not so nice and who, and correct me if this is wrong, never distinguished himself as antiwar, and so Iraq doesn't include Douglas, do we agree?"

"Well, he was for the nuclear freeze."

"*Who wasn't?* That was twenty years ago!"

She'd done all she could on that one.

He said, "When I first saw you, I thought you looked exactly like the pretty girl in profile they had with If You Can Draw This on matchbook covers to recruit art students . . ."

"You told me that. It was nice."

What could she do? He wasn't focusing at all, poor lamb. She said, "I have so many things I want to say to you—"

Ned said, his voice raised and not steady, "I know what I'll say if you die first, Nina. I know. I don't know what you'll say for me. I don't know. I know you'll be kind. I'm mixing things up. I'm sorry."

She got out of her chair and bent over him and stroked his neck. She said, "Oh, my guy, just put two things in front of you. Whatever he was, this man, your friend, lost half of his mortal life. People who depended on him are suffering. He had attainments—"

Ned said, "You're going to outlive me, by the stats." He was wrenching it out of himself. She fell to her knees in front of him, embracing him.

"Are you trying to destroy me?" she said.

"No. And I know you don't want to hear it, but we did something I still think is very funny. We got a bumper sticker printed up at a place on Mott Street. It said, HONK IF YOU LOVE JESUS. DON'T IF YOU DON'T. I'm not going to mention it, I'm just telling you."

"Well I think that's funny, too. Look at me. You can just stand up and say what it was like when you knew him as a friend, forget everything since, just what he meant to you at that time, and that you're sorry he's dead, this mixed creature, like all of us, and you honor his good works. And then you sit down. *Look* at me. And swear to me that you are going to leave out all your murmurings about the connection between personal death and social death and so on into the night. Swear to me."

He nodded. She inhaled extravagantly. They sat watching cloud shadows on the distant hills.

52 Nina said, "Since we've been here, I get a shiver sometimes when you're talking, like when I realize the tree I've been admiring is really a cell phone mast disguised as a pine tree. Or it's like your voice is dubbed for a minute. And then you come back. Now you're back."

"Nervousness," he said. Nina was eating raisins from a little box.

The striped tent they were in was enormous. A steady

wind was blowing, surging at times. The tent walls bulged in or out at intervals. The crowd filled the tent. Coir matting had been rolled out across the sodden grass. Lights, cameras, and microphones were concentrated toward the front of the space. There was a director. There was a printed program. The friends, except for Elliot, were in the front-row reserved section. Ned had told Nina she shouldn't be talking to him too much, but she kept bringing things up. He wanted her to stop counting the crowd. It didn't matter if there were two hundred or two hundred and fifty, did it?

He was looking at Iva, who was seated in a high-backed gothic chair. She was at the center of the row of notables behind the podium where he would be standing soon enough. Iva did look markedly happier, which went along with the latest from Jacques, who had intercepted them as they entered the tent to report that the critical part of the great settlement/deal with the powers that be had gone through very suddenly, overjoying Iva and Elliot. Iva was resplendent in what Nina had described as a Restoration wench mourning gown. It was true that she was showing a certain amount of flesh. A question that was never asked was, Why are you staring at that naked babe? was something Douglas had said. Joris was on Ned's left. He had his eyes closed. Gruen was on Joris's left.

Ah, death, Ned thought. Probably he would have to fight Nina to get her to promise no ceremony for him, when his time came. He'd never been to a funeral he liked. He felt cranky. It was Ronald Reagan who said Beware of empty hoopla.

Iva was doing something unattractive, which was to

straighten her arm and pluck at the loose flesh on her elbow. Nina had pointed out that Iva did this when she was excited.

He was, he felt, attending reasonably well to the proceedings despite thinking about himself too much. A woman was singing "Für Elise," accompanied by a CD. It was a song that always drew him into negative thoughts. He took Nina's hand. He was convinced that she was pregnant. Children hated having old parents, and their child would have one old parent and one not old, and that would be the best he could do for the little creature. The Israeli consul general for Newark had gone on interminably. According to Jacques, there were numbers of what he called *plainclothes Israelis* around the premises, some of them removing cartons from the tower basement. He was going to break Nina's heart, but he would strongly prefer not to see Jacques, with his black headband, ever again, not even in his charming caravan *in a cowfield* in Lyon. The consul general had said too much but the representative of the Ligues des droits de l'homme had said almost nothing. Ned knew who he was. He was a personal hero of Ned's.

There was a shuffling going on in the audience. The feet of the metal folding chairs were sinking unevenly into the matting as it absorbed water.

He was on next. Then it would be Gruen and Joris reading what had been given them, like zombies, despite having said they wouldn't. For a funerary event there should be something like a black tent available, not this festive entity they were in.

Ned saw with surprise that Hume had taken a seat at the end of the line of notables. He was wearing a suit and tie. There was nothing to complain about in the matter of his grooming, thanks to Nina. Ned was relieved, greatly.

The director beckoned. Ned made his way to the podium. Nina was insane. She had half risen when he got up. She had almost come with him.

He had tears in his eyes even before he began. He gave his name.

He said, "Douglas Delmarter was my friend years ago when I was a student, when we were students, at NYU. When he was young he had the idea he could force the world to be funny, or funnier than it intended to be. I think he needed it to be funnier for his own reasons, or actually for his own needs. I have no idea what those were. He was a secretive person even then. But anyway, as a fixation . . . it fascinated me. I am speaking for myself here. I allowed it to cheer me up and I was at a point when I needed cheering up. Later he gave up needling the world in this way and switched to trying to figure out the Why side of things, the Why does the world feel so wrong? side of it. In any case, he went on to honorable and impressive acts, deeds, in fact, about which we have heard much today.

"I'm very sorry that my friend is dead, and dead when he was hardly through with what he might have done.

"You may be wondering what the book is that I'm holding. It's Douglas's paperback copy of Boswell's *Life of Samuel Johnson*.

"Douglas loved this book. It was probably the best reading recommendation to us, his friends, that he made, and he made many. In fact he loved the damn thing so much he stopped reading it at page 847 in order to save the experience of finishing it for some celebratory high moment he assumed would come, some moment greater and happier than any so far.

"What I am going to do is read aloud a page or so for the benefit of our friend's spirit. It may be a little strange because one of Douglas's many positions was that anyone who believed in the afterlife should be barred from seeking political office. So, my old friend, this is for your soul, whose survival is, as you used to say in Wallace Bray's philosophy class, highly suppository. I hope you can hear this, Douglas.

"This is where Douglas stopped reading. And these are the words he would have read next. This, of course, is Boswell speaking. I'm starting halfway down page 847:

> I had learnt from Dr. Johnson during this interview,
> not to think with a dejected indifference of the
> works of art, and the pleasures of life, because
> life is uncertain and short; but to consider such
> indifference as a failure of reason, a morbidness of
> mind; for happiness should be cultivated as much
> as we can, and the objects which are instrumental
> should be steadily considered as of importance, with
> a reference not only to ourselves, but to multitudes
> in successive ages. Though it is proper to value small
> parts, as 'Sands make the mountain, moments make
> the year,' yet we must contemplate, collectively, to
> have a just estimation of objects. One moment's
> being uneasy or not, seems of no consequence; yet
> this may be thought of the next, and the next, and so
> on, til there is a large portion of misery. In the same
> way one must think of happiness, of learning, of

friendship. We cannot tell the precise moment when friendship is formed . . ."

Ned pressed the tears from his eyes with a ball of tissue. He hesitated, and returned to his seat.

February 15, 2003

53 He would never forget this day. He felt clean. The march column was twenty-five across and it was disciplined. The column had a sense of itself. *A day of streets like rivers of fists* was a survivor from earlier wars, earlier protests, but now it was real, in San Francisco, on Market Street. The sun had been a bright smear in the overcast but it had come out, whole, shining brilliantly on their efforts. Thousands of people had come to the city, thousands. He thought again, It makes you feel clean. Whenever the forward movement of the column halted, the marchers spontaneously linked arms and then maintained that as long as was practicable, which wasn't long, really, because some people in any rank would move at a slower pace than the majority. There were two wheelchair battalions, he knew, somewhere. He wanted to inhale more deeply than it was physically possible to. The lead cohort of the march was a mile or more ahead of where he was, unbelievably. He had been up with the dignitaries and they were going to mention his name at Union Square, at the rally, but he had decided to fade back deeper into the march. He didn't want to arrive. He wanted to continue to feel the march.

Someone had put an extension ladder up against a first-story overhang above a German restaurant. It looked safe enough. He wanted to be up there where he'd be able to see so much more. There were maybe twenty people on the overhang already, some shaking their signs at a TV truck that was trying to pierce the column at a cross street.

There was no obstacle to mounting the ladder, so he did. He stepped out onto the overhang. It was a fantasy of goodwill. The feeder streets were jammed with participants waiting to join the main body of the march. He shook hands with the other people on the roof. There were Japanese tourists among them, very shy. A black high school step dance group that was part of the march was drawing enormous cheers from the thick crowds along the sidewalks. We never get enough black people out, so we love the ones who do come, he thought. He cheered as hard as he could, himself.

I love every moment of my life that has brought me here, he thought. They were going to stop the fuckers. One of the Japanese had a transistor radio. What was happening here was happening across the world. BBC was saying ten to fifteen million in all the capitals, the greatest march numbers in fucking human history *ever*. Berlin, Paris, London, had already reported and the numbers had been astounding. He thought, Today we are treading on the corpse of this war.

People in the march were saluting as though the overhang were a reviewing stand. He wanted to shout something juvenile, like Every hand being raised in this march is grasping the hand of a person who will not die because of us. He wanted the march to suck the occupants out of every building as it passed, and leave them empty.

He thought, You can't control everything. He couldn't control Nina. She was with one of the Berkeley women's groups. She was pregnant and he had briefly thought he could get her on one of the ludicrous but earnest floats that were part of the parade, but she had laughed at him. They had their cell phones and would find each other at Union Square. Being on a float was still being part of the march and he couldn't see why it had been such a bad idea for her.

Everything was good. He had a rising feeling in his chest like nothing he had ever felt. The signs could use improvement. Some of Douglas's inventions would have made good signs, like War Is the Continuation of Business as Usual by Any Means Necessary, and Strike When the Gorgon Blinks. They were too literary, but still.

Everything was good. Two exile Cuban anarchist groups that had been fighting forever were marching together under a common banner saying Frente Libertario. *Go*, old men! he wanted to shout. He knew some of them. Maybe one or two of them might notice him there. He waved violently. He went right to the parapet to try to signal his presence. Their eyesight might not be up to it. Racially, everything was okay and looking better. It had been Nina's idea to contact the step dance teams in the black high schools. There was a huge contingent from McClymonds. He wanted to be everywhere in the march. Except with the drum groups, which were unbearably loud. He felt drunk with gratitude and the conviction of victory. He thought, You can't control everything . . . but this we can control. There would be no war. In part because of them there would be no war in Iraq. A few new people had come onto the overhang and he was going to shake hands with them, too. There would be no war. He thought, No war, No invasion, No.

ACKNOWLEDGMENTS

With deep gratitude to both my editor Ann Close and my agent Andrew Wylie, and with affection for both. And with thanks for the encouragement and astute suggestions supplied by early readers of this book—my beloved brothers Nick and Chris, Mona Simpson, Tom Hayes, Joshua Pashman, Leslie McGrath, Max Porter. My old friend Tom Disch would have been on this list, but for outrageous fortune.

Norman Rush grew up in Oakland, California, and graduated from Swarthmore College in 1956. He is the author of three previous works of fiction: *Whites*, a collection of stories, and two novels, *Mating* and *Mortals*. His stories have appeared in *The New Yorker*, *The Paris Review*, and *Best American Short Stories*. *Mating* was the recipient of the National Book Award. Rush and his wife live in Rockland County, New York.

A NOTE ON THE TYPE

This book was set in Caledonia, a typeface designed by W. A. Dwiggins (1880–1956). It belongs to the family of printing types called "modern face" by printers—a term used to mark the change in style of the type letters that occurred around 1800. Caledonia borders on the general design of Scotch Roman but it is more freely drawn than that letter. This version of Caledonia was adapted by David Berlow in 1979.

COMPOSED BY
North Market Street Graphics, Lancaster, Pennsylvania

PRINTED AND BOUND BY
RR Donnelly, Harrisonburg, Pennsylvania

DESIGNED BY
Iris Weinstein